ABOVE
THE BRIDGE

A Paige MacKenzie Mystery

Deborah Garner

Cranberry Cove Press

Above the Bridge
by Deborah Garner

Copyright © 2014 Deborah Garner
ALL RIGHTS RESERVED

First Printing – April 2014
ISBN: 978-0-9960449-0-5

This is a work of fiction. Names, characters, places and incidents either are products of the author's imagination or used fictitiously. Any resemblance to actual events or locales or persons, living or dead, is entirely coincidental.

Printed in the U.S.A.

For My Father

CHAPTER ONE

Just before midnight, Paige Mackenzie walked to the door of her room, twisted the cool, metal knob and stepped outside. She glanced around the half-filled parking lot and vacant sidewalk, peered up and down the street at the dark windows of nearby stores and leaned back against the inside of the door frame. Taking a deep breath, she exhaled slowly, a frosty cloud of white slinking away from her lips and out into the late October night.

Looking up, she watched the moonlight dissipate softly across the cloudless sky. It had been that way for several nights. As with each recent evening, she stood under the ceiling of stars and felt a gentle peace settle over her, one of many welcome changes in her life.

It had been almost a week since Paige had arrived in the western mountains of Wyoming. And it had taken her that long just to begin accepting the quiet nature of the area, a jolt of a change from her hectic New York life. She had spent the previous week driving across the country, slowly leaving the Atlantic coast and eastern life behind her.

Wyoming had been a shock to Paige. The open land seemed to go on forever and the highways stretched endlessly into the distance. Crossing the state from the east, the open fields had encouraged her mind to wander. Each mile she covered had made the next one feel even more welcome. Though she was traveling with a purpose, she knew any geographic change had the potential of kicking up the unexpected.

She had stumbled into Jackson on a late Friday afternoon, finding a room in town at the Sweet Mountain Inn. She'd dropped her overnight bag on the bed and set up her toothbrush, toothpaste and favorite lavender soap on the narrow, glass shelf in the bathroom. The last leg of her trip had been long and tiring, five hundred miles from Denver in one straight shot. The previous day's drive had been just as taxing, another five hundred mile stretch from Topeka to Denver. It was tempting to collapse on the bed and rest. But curiosity outweighed exhaustion and the lure of the unfamiliar town called out to her.

Fighting fatigue, she'd cupped her hands under the bathroom faucet and splashed cold water on her face. A look in the mirror confirmed what she suspected. She looked as tired as she felt. Her eyes, usually a sparkling green, appeared dull and lifeless. She turned her head slightly to the side, noting, as she had many times before, that she'd inherited her father's nose and strong jaw line, along with her mother's smooth skin and high cheekbones. Running a brush quickly through her auburn hair, she set out to explore.

Sauntering slowly down the main street, she'd let first impressions of the town sink in. Store windows displayed western wear, cowboy hats and impressively realistic wildlife sculptures. Upscale galleries showcased exquisite photographic works, while jewelry store windows framed unique, one of a kind, artist creations. Smaller shops sold homemade candies, ice cream, local huckleberry jam and fresh roasted coffee beans, as well as a hefty assortment of souvenirs for the multitude of tourists the area attracted.

She had paused to order a vanilla latte to go from a small coffee house, hidden away in an old log cabin on a side street, a sign above the door announcing it as The Blue Sky Café. Adding a raspberry-orange muffin to her purchase, she'd continued to wander through town, arriving finally at the town square. On a park bench, surrounded by trees and attractive landscaping, she'd begun to contemplate the possibilities her visit might hold. Though not yet defined, they felt endless.

Now, on this cold, crisp night, her back pressed against the solid wooden door frame, thoughts tumbled around in her mind, just as they had on that very first day. What had brought her to the west, to Jackson Hole in particular? She'd been given a fair amount of latitude in choosing a location to research. A trip down the Atlantic coast would have certainly been easier, but it was something she had done many times before. She'd always managed to keep from wandering but now, at the age of thirty-four, she knew she was ready to step outside the familiar.

Susan was always good about listening to Paige's input, which was something Paige appreciated about her editor. She'd been a little surprised that Paige had chosen to distance herself so far from familiar territory, yet the more they had discussed various options, the more Susan had felt that Paige's proposal was feasible. It had been some time since the paper had done a story on anything outside of the immediate region. It made sense that the east coast readership would be drawn to a story about a western Wyoming area. Jackson Hole had seemed a good choice.

Paige stepped back inside, eased the door closed and listened for the click of the latch. Out of habit, she locked both the doorknob and the deadbolt above it, though she was aware many residents of the area didn't lock their doors at all.

It was just one of many differences she'd noticed upon her arrival.

Other differences included the slow pace of life, the way people took their time to explain things, the patient attitudes they had when listening. Cars stopped at crosswalks and horns didn't honk the split second traffic lights turned green. The few traffic lights there were, that is. Merchants weren't afraid to accept local checks. Strangers weren't greeted with looks of suspicion. It appeared in this town that people were actually innocent until proven otherwise, a proof that apparently was rarely necessary, according to the almost nonexistent crime rate. Within these observations Paige had begun to breathe a little easier, to relax into the calm peace of the mountain town.

It was during the first few days after arriving in Jackson, maybe four, maybe five, that Paige noticed Jake. She'd taken her usual place in line at the Blue Sky Café, right behind another regular she recognized as a woman who wore a different hat each day and right before Old Man Thompson. At least that was what Maddie, who ran the popular, funky café, called him.

Paige was stirring sugar and cinnamon into her sturdy paper cup, clutching the heat-protecting wrap with her free hand and watching Maddie hand Old Man Thompson a plain bagel, toasted well, with light butter, just the way he'd ordered it the morning before. And the morning before that. She had just tapped the edge of her spoon on her cup and was reaching to deposit it into a glass marked for used spoons when a jingle of bells on the front door caught her attention. Glancing over her shoulder, she first saw the weathered cowboy hat, tilted slightly to the left of a fine-chiseled face. A bit sun-kissed, Paige thought, most likely from working outside. Faded blue jeans and a red and blue plaid shirt blended in with the hat and tanned complexion. A scuffed pair of brown boots peered out from below the jeans.

"Hey, Jake," Maddie shouted across the counter. "What'll it be today? Black coffee and a cinnamon roll? Or black coffee and a blueberry scone? Or black coffee and black coffee?"

The man she called Jake took a few strides over to the counter, his boots clicking against the old, wooden floor.

"You know me too well, Maddie, old girl," he said with a slight smile. "Black coffee and black coffee it is."

"Who're you calling an old girl," Maddie said, holding back the coffee as Jake shook his head and laughed.

"Maddie, you look younger to me every day," he crooned, "I wake up each morning and just can barely wait to get here and see you and your pretty face." He raised both of his hands and smacked them against his own face for emphasis.

"Take your coffee, you sweet talker, you," Maddie replied, waving away his outstretched money and signaling the next customer to move up in the line, a slight woman who had entered just after Jake.

Taking a seat in the corner, Paige grabbed a copy of the local paper and tried to bury herself in the morning news. A stark contrast from The New York Times that consistently landed on her doorstep each morning at home, this paper was filled with stories unique to the immediate area. A wildlife conservation group was protesting newly increased hunting quotas. The town council had turned down a proposal for a major commercial remodel, based on blueprints that detailed building heights that were well above those allowed by the planning commission. A few pages into the paper, an impressive list of musical appearances stretched down the right side of the crisp newsprint. It was clear the town's new Center for the Arts pulled in big names.

"I'd try to get tickets for Willie Nelson if I were you," a woman passing by the table said, noticing Paige looking over the event section of the publication. "He was amazing the last time he was here. If it's sold out, try for Bob Dylan. Or Joan Armatrading." Paige offered a quick thank you as the woman scooted out the door.

Between articles, she found herself sneaking glances at Jake, who had taken a seat in a small, corner booth on the opposite side of the cafe. He was attractive; there was no doubt about it. But she was here for work, she reminded herself. Besides, it had been a year since her last relationship ended and she'd grown accustomed to having her time to herself. As a side benefit, it certainly made it easier to focus on work and finish assignments without distraction.

Jake slid back in the booth and swirled his coffee around in his cup. He reached over to a wire rack by the wall and pulled a copy of the local paper from the top of a pile. Again he swirled his coffee, took a sip, thumbed through the paper, took another sip, followed it with another swirl, and finally stood, folded the paper under his arm, and walked out the front door. He'd never glanced up at Paige.

Two days later Paige saw Jake again. She'd stopped in at a local mountaineering store in search of a sturdy flashlight for her car. While comparing a budget priced, hefty red one with a pricier, slender, metallic blue model, she caught a glimpse of the back of Jake's hat and then recognized the click of the boots. He held an armful of supplies: colorful ropes, a pick axe and an assortment of metal clips. Climbing equipment, from what she could tell. No wonder he was in such good shape, she mused, fighting back a smile.

She chose the blue flashlight and browsed around for a few minutes. Numerous customers arrived, drawn in by end-of-season sale signs. The store stocked a wide variety of items; it wasn't hard to see why it was popular. Backpacks of all sizes, shapes and colors hung from hooks on one wall, their straps and ties dangling down. Running shoes, hiking boots and sandals filled another section. Tents and sleeping bags made up a center display. A rack near the check-out counter was packed with insect repellants, tubes of sunscreen and canisters of bear spray.

"Quite an assortment you have here," Paige commented as she placed the flashlight on the counter.

"Yep," the young clerk quipped, a boy hardly out of his teens. "What you need just depends on what you're planning to do. Lots of outdoor activities around here."

"So I see," Paige nodded, glancing around at the racks one more time.

"Take that guy who just left. New in town. Obsessed with mountain climbing." The clerk ran the flashlight over a flash of red light, entering the sale into the store register.

"You planning on doing any rafting?" he continued. "You might need a waterproof jacket."

"No. I'm just here to do some writing. I'll only be here a few weeks at most." Paige rummaged through her wallet for cash.

"Well, at least get yourself a strong sunscreen," the clerk advised. "This altitude can be tough on skin. Wise to have some protection against those rays."

Following his advice, Paige added a high-level SPF sun block to her flashlight purchase, paid the cashier and left.

The third time she saw Jake was two days later, this time at the farmer's market on the town square. Same hat, same boots, different armful of supplies, this time corn, apples, a loaf of bread, a small jar of what might have been jam or honey and half a dozen other items that Paige couldn't recognize from her position at the flower cart. Armed with sunflowers and a basket of raspberries, she watched him briefly as he moved on to another vendor. Somewhere between a table offering homemade tamales and a green van selling sacks of freshly harvested potatoes, Jake slipped off through the crowd and disappeared. Paige finished her shopping, gathered her purchases, and headed back to the inn.

It was a brief article on an inner page of the local paper the next morning that helped Paige start to put the pieces together. Jake Norris, originally from Cody, but a newcomer to Jackson, had bought the old historic Manning ranch, about fifteen miles north of town. Twenty-six acres, with magnificent views of the Grand Tetons, a huge barn, six small cabins, a two-story farmhouse and plenty of room for cattle and horses to graze.

The ranch had been on the market for many years, becoming increasingly run down as time went on. Many potential new owners had looked at the property, but a sale had never been finalized. Some prospective buyers had edged away, perhaps because legend had it that the ranch had been built on old Native American burial grounds. It had also long been rumored that at least the farmhouse was haunted, if not other buildings on the land, as well. Undoubtedly, others had stepped back because it was just too darn expensive, like most of the real estate in the area. Jake Norris had watched it calmly as the price continued to drop slightly with each deal that fell through, moving in at the last minute with an acceptable offer.

Paige set the paper down, poured another cup of fresh ground coffee and looked out the window of her room, running the details of the article over in her mind. A ranch with a mysterious history could make for intriguing reading. Burial grounds and haunted buildings would certainly draw interest, but she would need specifics. Perhaps there were multiple accounts of unusual activity on the property. Or maybe the rumors had merely started up when the ranch stayed on the market for an extended period of time. It was doubtful that there would be enough to go on, but it was worth keeping the ranch in mind.

The light outside dimmed, causing Paige to look up towards the sky. Where there had been mere wisps of clouds just an hour before, there were now thick, gray pillows, growing more solid and closer to each other by the minute. This wasn't surprising to Paige, who was already becoming used to the weather's constant changes. But if she planned to head out at all, she knew she should do it soon.

Standing in front of a small assortment of hanging clothes on the rack in her room, she grabbed a black turtleneck top and her favorite jeans. She'd brought very little clothing with her, leaving most of her wardrobe back home. Still, not knowing the exact length of her stay, she'd played it safe and packed a bit of everything, leaning towards the casual side. Now she reached forward again and ran her fingers across the tops of the hangers, landing finally on a hunter green jacket. It was a favorite of hers, with its soft fleece lining, matching hood and spacious pockets. She pulled it off the hanger and slipped it on quickly, grabbing her car keys and an umbrella on her way out the door.

The drive north from Jackson was an easy one. For one thing, there was only one road out of town in that direction, making it essentially impossible to get lost. And once Paige left the activity of the town itself behind, the road opened up, curving alongside the vast expanse of the National Elk Refuge on the right and passing the impressive National Museum of Wildlife Art on the left, a stunning building of native rock that blended into the butte so naturally that it almost seemed possible it had evolved geologically, as had the valley itself. There were very few other cars on the road and one by one, they peeled off alongside the shoulder to take photos of the wide landscape vistas or to pose with other family members in front of the entrance sign to Grand Teton National Park. It wasn't long before Paige found she had the highway to herself.

Even having read descriptions of the Grand Tetons in her pre-trip research, nothing could have prepared her for her first glimpse of the mountain range. Seeing the sloping butte fall away to the left and the spectacular peaks of the Tetons rise up in the distance took her breath away with a sudden, intense punch. As if to boast about their soaring heights above the valley floor, the highest peaks wore crowns of the previous winter's snow, a sharp contrast to the October terrain below.

Paige continued driving north. Fading blooms of Indian Paintbrush and scrubby stretches of sagebrush lined the sides of the road. The Jackson Hole Airport appeared in the distance, blending so uniformly with the landscape that, had it not been for the single rise of a control tower, it could easily have been missed from the road. It faded away behind her after she passed the airport junction, marked with a simple, rustic brown signpost. In the rear view mirror she saw a small shuttle bus turn out of the airport driveway and head south towards town. It struck Paige as inconceivable that the small, unobtrusive transportation hub for the area could handle the massive volume that it did.

She focused her attention on the road before her, glancing occasionally at the open fields on both sides of the highway.   Bison grazed to her right, clusters of hefty mammals hovering together, a few younger members of the herd standing close to their mothers. A red fox played in the field to her left, sprinting, crouching and then freezing in place to wait patiently for unsuspecting rodents to show their faces. It didn't take long for the fox to pounce forward and come up away from the earth with a dinner appetizer.

Paige turned off the main highway, taking a right turn onto Antelope Flats Road. Heading east, away from the Tetons, the road meandered around the historic structures of Mormon Row. She had read about this area while doing research. The group of preserved buildings dated back to the early 1900's, when predominantly Mormon pioneers settled in the valley. Continuing on, Paige turned south, following the road to the small town of Kelly. Set off to the south side of the road, the sparsely populated town appeared to hold not much more than a handful of cabins, yurts and other modest forms of housing. As far as Paige could see, there were no sizable commercial establishments to sell groceries or other necessities, though a small eatery offered coffee and sandwiches. The town clearly depended on Jackson itself to provide a source for most of its supplies.

Paige veered to the right as the road curved west, placing the Tetons directly in front of her. Again, the soaring peaks of the mountain range astonished her. They dwarfed everything around them. Even the sizable buttes in the valley seemed meager in comparison.

Not long after passing the small Kelly post office on the edge of town, she spotted a work shed along the south side of the road, a few pieces of rustic furniture scattered in front. She pulled off the road, feeling the car bounce beneath her as it navigated potholes in the unpaved driveway. She parked the car, stepped out onto the dusty ground and took a look around.   A tall easel stood to the left of the building's doorway, displaying photographs of pine bed frames, sturdy dining tables and rustic chairs, all artistically handcrafted from logs. Twisted bundles of slender tree branches framed mirrors of varying sizes. The designs were elegant in their simplicity, but also creative and woodsy. These were not the cookie cutter designs that she had seen in a few of the more tourist-oriented stores downtown.   Several of the pieces were appealing enough that Paige began to wonder if some new furniture might be in order, hard as it would be to ship it back to the east coast.

The sound of approaching footsteps interrupted Paige's imaginary home redecorating.   Looking up, she spotted a man in well-worn, dusty work clothes stepping into view from behind the shed.   He appeared to be in his mid-seventies, a sturdy fellow with a face that spoke of decades of hard work.   He nodded a friendly greeting as he drew closer, brushing sawdust from his shirt sleeves at the same time.   A large black Labrador trotted alongside him, his tail wagging an additional welcome.

"Can I help ya?" he called from about ten yards away. "Dan here. Dan McElroy. These are my creations."   He waved his hand towards the pictures on the easel and then immediately signaled Paige to follow him to the side of the small building.

A tall, red barn with a pitched roof stood about fifty yards behind the smaller wood shed.   Paige walked across to the barn, following a few steps behind Dan.   She looked up at the tall, sliding door with faded, peeling paint on crisscrossed wood planks, pushed a few small rocks out of her way and stepped inside.

A lengthy work table ran along the right side of the barn wall.   A table saw sat on one end, a corresponding pile of sawdust on the floor below it. Assorted bins of nails and screws sat in various spots on the work counter and a pegboard holding old tools hung from the wall above the work space. Tall piles of lodgepole pine were stacked around the floor, divided into several batches according to size. Across the barn, scattered pieces of furniture stood in partial stages of completion – a long, rectangular table, a set of outdoor patio chairs, staircase sets of bookshelves and other semi-finished projects.

"What brings you to these parts?" Dan asked, looking back over his shoulder, while reaching for a hammer from the pegboard. He grabbed an assortment of nails from one of the bins, crouched down alongside the rectangular table, and drove a nail into the side of a rustic leg.

"I'm here to do some research for an article for the Manhattan Post," Paige offered, watching how careful Dan was to work the nails in with precision. She glanced upward, figuring the roof must be at least fifty feet tall. Small rays of light shone through the cracks, casting a surreal glow around the rest of the interior.

"You're a writer, then," the man mused. "I've known a few of your like in my day. Sometimes nice folks, sometimes trouble." Paige thought she saw him cast a wink in her direction, but wasn't entirely sure. He continued to set nails into the wooden legs of the table, moving from one to another in a counter-clockwise direction.

"What's your article about?" Dan asked, without missing a stroke of the hammer. Paige noticed he was wearing a tan, leather vest, with a few tassels of fringe hanging from the hem. As he moved with the hammer, the thin, leather pieces swayed in the air, dangling like windy branches on a willow tree.

"I'm not entirely sure," Paige admitted. "But it needs to have some sort of western angle, so the paper decided to feature Jackson Hole. I figured if I could get a sense of the area's history first-hand, the rest might follow."

Dan laughed out loud. "You big city folk always crack me up. Thinking you can mosey on in and breathe up a dose of western heritage. Ain't that easy, ma'am. But I wish you luck anyway." Dan seemed to pause for a moment, staring at the last nail he had set, inspecting the results of the final hammer stroke he had made. Then he stood, straightened up to his full height, which Paige estimated to be over six feet, and stared at the table for a minute. He turned slowly to face Paige.

"There's a lot that's gone on in this area that people don't know about," he said cautiously. "Well, some people do, some people don't." He paused a few seconds, as if to consider what he had said. "There's a whole lotta secrets in this valley. The ones people talk about aren't so much true. It's the ones people don't mention too often that can get a person wondering."

Paige pondered this for a minute, not sure how to respond. Maybe these were just the musings of a man who lived a quiet life and spent his time alone making furniture, with too much time to let his imagination run wild. But then again, maybe there were secrets hidden in Jackson Hole that even many of the residents didn't know. Maybe she'd stumbled into something bigger than the mere history lesson she'd expected.

"You'll see, if you stick around long enough and keep your eyes open and ears alert," Dan said, watching her as if he could read her thoughts. "Are you just here for a short bit? Or planning to spend some time in our beautiful valley?"

Paige took a look around her. Beautiful it was, there was no question about that. Looking through the barn's doorway and gazing across the valley, the mountains rose up like monuments to heaven, stretching into the clouds, mist wrapping around the upper peaks. As if to accentuate the drama of the view, a lone bald eagle soared across the sky, landing regally in a tree not far from the barn. The air was clean, crisp and cool and the smell of the woodwork mixed with the scent of late fall.

"I'll be around for a little while, however long it takes to finish the article," Paige said, half to Dan and half to herself, as she watched the eagle take flight again.

Dan's words had piqued her curiosity. Maybe there were more elusive stories in the valley than she had originally expected to find. Her goal in coming out to Jackson Hole had simply been to tie local culture and western history into an enjoyable article for readers. But Dan had inadvertently hinted at something better. If a more unique story could be found, it would give her a better angle, which was never a bad thing. It would take perseverance and, most likely, a bit of luck to search it out, but it would be well worth it. If it even existed at all, she reminded herself. And if it all took longer than she'd originally planned, she was starting to think she wouldn't mind. It had only taken a few days to grow fond of the area.

"You got a place to stay, city-slicker?" Dan asked, arms folded now, weight shifted onto one leg, hip slightly swayed.

"I've got a room at the Sweet Mountain Inn," Paige replied. "Not much space, but it's reasonable and clean. Right in the center of town, easy to get around. At least I have it for the next day or two. They may be booked up after that, but there are other places to stay in town. Many of them, it seems, just looking up and down a few blocks."

Dan laughed. "You're right about that. We probably have more hotels, motels, inns and lodges in Jackson Hole than you do back there in New York City." Pausing, he added, "OK, I doubt that's entirely true. Besides, I've never been east of Nebraska. But we sure do have a lot."

"I think you must need them," Paige commented, remembering an article she'd seen in the local paper the day before. "You guys get almost four million people coming through here each year. That's pretty amazing for a town with a population of only nine thousand or so."

"That many, you say?" Dan said, stopping briefly to take this in. "I don't know about statistics and that kind of stuff, but I've gone into town during the summer months and there's sure not much room to walk down the sidewalks. I try to stay out here as much as I can. That's one good thing; you don't have to get far out of town to find a little peace and quiet."

Dan looked around appreciatively at the open fields around him before continuing.

"Well, if you decide you need a little more privacy or room to breathe, I've got a cabin I rent sometimes. Not very fancy, but plenty quiet. Might be good for a writer type such as yourself." Dan pushed the table a bit to the side, took a cue from Paige's silence and waved her over to the door of the barn. She followed him, both out of politeness and curiosity.

Outside, Dan pointed across a nondescript field to a small log structure at the edge of his property. It had a narrow porch, a modest front door, two rustic windows, and a slightly sloping roof with a short chimney on top. Paige took a look at it, not failing to notice the dramatic mountain backdrop.

"If you're gonna be here at least a little while, I rent it by the week. Only sometimes, and I never advertise it. Rather have it empty than have some wacko stranger in it." Dan sighed and shook his head, undoubtedly remembering at least one undesirable tenant. "But you seem like a nice lady. You think about it. I've had writers in there before, they say it's a good place to think and get the words out, or whatever it is you writers do. Like I said, you think about it. Eighty bucks a week, in advance. Business is slow right now. Could help me out and help you, too."

Paige stood silent for a minute. She hadn't intended to take on regular rent. She wasn't even sure how long she would stay. And the people who ran the Sweet Mountain Inn were wonderful and had been very accommodating since she'd arrived. But they had also warned her that there were a few nights coming up that were already booked solid. She might be forced to find other lodging if she needed to stay. In addition, it seemed there was something calling to her in this valley, though she couldn't pinpoint what it was. The chance of finding good story, perhaps, or just a needed break from city life. She hadn't taken a vacation in years.

"You know, I might be interested," Paige said slowly. "Mind if I take a look at it?"

"Help yourself. Door's open. Go on in and look around all you want. It's not too fancy, being as it was built back in the early 1900's. But it's got running water and electricity now. You know, electricity didn't come to this area until 1921," Dan added quickly, looking quite proud of himself for knowing this fact. "It has a small bath and a nice little fireplace. If you decide you're interested, I can throw a bed and table in there for you. Maybe a couple other spare pieces of furniture. You look around, let me know." Dan twisted his neck to the side, making it crack sharply. He turned and headed back into the barn.

Paige looked over at the cabin. It wouldn't hurt to take a look around, even if just to see the inside of an historic dwelling and get a feeling for the way the early pioneers had lived. She headed across the field and approached the small, rustic building.

The porch was narrow, maybe six feet deep, running the width of the building, which Paige approximated to be around fifteen feet across. A patchy roof slanted out and downward above the porch. Similar to those inside the barn, rays of light peeked through the slats in the porch roof. An old, metal tub rested on the floor, just to the right of the door. A few dried flowers lingered in the tub's dirt, left over from the warmer summer weather.

Slowly Paige turned the handle on the door and pushed it open. It was dark, but enough light entered through the windows to be able to make out the interior. There were two rooms, one in front and a second directly behind it. A small bathroom sat off to the right of the front room. There was no kitchen, but she could see a narrow, wooden counter and small sink on the far left wall. A cupboard hung above those, the door open to reveal empty shelves.

The main room wasn't large, but the sloping roof helped it feel more spacious. In addition to the two windows in front, a side window faced west towards the Tetons, which meant there would be good afternoon light. In the far corner was a small, rock fireplace, with a wide hearth and a few fireplace tools beside it in a metal bucket. With each October night seeming colder than the one before, a warm fire wouldn't be a bad way to end the day, Paige mused.

The back room was identical to the front, though not quite as deep. Paige approximated it to be about eight by fifteen feet. It was dark, with just one small window centered high on the east wall. There was ample room for a bed and a dresser, though not much more than that. A throw rug could be tossed on the worn, wooden floors to add color and, Paige thought with amusement, a little warmth to go with her habit of staying barefoot most of the time. There was no closet, but a few small hooks poked out from alongside the window, which would allow her to hang up a few articles of clothing. Two shelves hung above the hooks, a perfect place for folded shirts and sweaters.

Dan was outside the barn, sawing a slender piece of lodgepole pine into smaller pieces, when Paige walked back from the cabin. Two sawhorses swayed slightly with each movement of his hand saw. Not far away, the black lab had curled up in the shade of a cottonwood tree and was attentively supervising the work.

"I'll take it," she heard herself say impulsively, knowing she was acting purely on instinct.

Dan reached out with a quick handshake, immediately returning to finish sawing through the last inch of a three foot stretch of wood.

"It's a done deal," he said. "You can drop the first week's payment off whenever you want, today, tomorrow, whatever works for you. Oh – and there's no key. Don't worry; you won't need one out here. There's a latch on the inside of the door, though."

Paige looked around, summing up her new surroundings. Adding one impulse to another, she tossed out a question for Dan, keeping her voice as casual as possible.

"Do you happen to know where the old Manning ranch is?"

"That's an easy one," Dan replied, turning to face the road. "Head right up there a ways, past the fencepost at the end of the field and then around the curve to the left, just a little on down the road until you hit a right turn and then up the hill a bit, not too far but far enough. After that, take a left and then a right. You can't miss it."

"Nice place, that ranch," Dan added while lifting a log from a nearby stack to determine if it should be the next one to saw. "Run down, though, was abandoned a long time. Just recently bought up by a guy from Cody. Supposedly his family lived in that area back in the prospecting days. So they say."

Paige nodded a thank you, hoping she'd gotten enough of the country directions right to keep from getting lost. She promised to be back with the first week's rent and a few belongings the next day and set off in her car again, this time heading back in the direction of Kelly. A golden field stretched out to her left, two large bison resting in the middle. Wild thistle decorated the edge of the road, scattered about in tiny bursts of purple and brown. A magpie sat high on a fencepost at the end of the field, as if to signal that she was following Dan's directions so far.

Paige passed the field and found herself alongside a narrow, winding stream set off the road twenty yards or so. Tall reeds and muted, jewel-toned grasses grew along the water's edge. A bright yellow canoe rested upside down against the far bank. There was no fence separating the road from the water and a dusty, makeshift parking area marked this spot as an unofficial swimming hole.

Not more than another hundred yards beyond the stream, the road became increasingly narrow and began to climb. At first following only a slight incline, it quickly turned into a steeper grade, dipping periodically in roller coaster fashion. Finally, the road leveled out into a flat plateau, at which point Paige noticed a rustic barn in the distance, brown and weathered, surrounded by a handful of smaller buildings which were barely visible above the surrounding brush.

An impressive log gate stood alongside the road at the entrance of a narrow dirt driveway. Silhouettes of cowboys, wildlife and trees decorated the top of the arch, stretching overhead in a sculpted metal design. Small clusters of scrub brush dotted the surrounding landscape, alternating with taller bursts of dry grass.

Paige pulled her car up past the front gate, turned the wheel to the right and guided the vehicle over to the side of the road. She stepped out of the car quietly, feeling a slight breeze graze the side of her face. Leaving the car door only partially latched, she looked around, seeing only open stretches of land. This was what Dan meant about finding peace and quiet outside of town, Paige thought. As if in rebuttal, a crow above her let out a piercing screech before continuing its journey across the sky.

To the left of the driveway, a white metal sign with the words "No Trespassing" was nailed onto a fencepost. Faded and weathered as the sign was, the lettering made a clear enough statement. The property was off limits.

Paige walked to the barbed wire fence that ran alongside the entrance. There was no sign of anyone present on the land, at least not anyone she could see from where she stood. It was tempting to duck between the spiked wires and get a closer look at the property. She'd never been one to stay within the rules, a trait that had landed her in trouble more than once in her life. Still, her instincts told her not to push this time. She retreated to her car, paused to take in the overall view once more and then drove away, continuing east.

Paige followed the road a few more miles, winding into a canyon, where the landscape of trees thickened. Out of the corner of her eye, she spied a sudden movement within one particular cluster of trees. Pulling over quietly and peering through the foliage, she could make out the dark outline of a moose. Paige stepped cautiously out of the car and positioned herself at the side of the road, not close enough to be in danger, but close enough to clearly see the animal.

A few other cars passed by, passenger necks swiveling as the vehicles slowed down, something Paige would soon come to expect, the braking of cars to see why other cars on the road were stopping, all hoping to catch a glimpse of area wildlife. A young man stuck his head out of one car window and snapped a quick picture of the moose with a small point and shoot camera. A large motor home with blue horizontal pinstripes along the side yielded several tourists with cameras, who hopped out to take photographs from the side of the road.

Paige moved slowly around a small tree, resting against the bark and watching silently. Within a short time, the other onlookers returned to their vehicles and headed down the road. Paige remained behind, watching as the young moose meandered between trees and nibbled on branches and leaves, his fuzzy, newly-grown antlers not yet fully formed. Eventually the moose and Paige made eye contact, neither one moving, but letting their notice of each other linger silently in the autumn air. Determining that he was not threatened, the moose lowered his head and continued to munch on the local vegetation. Paige remained quiet and still.

Somewhere within these moments of silence, Paige realized she had stumbled into an adventure far beyond the scope of her assignment. Many miles from home, in a land of exquisite beauty, she had found a place to soak in a renewal of sorts. She'd discovered an environment that was conducive to examining her own life. A new purpose for her trip began to form in her mind and heart, one that had the potential to carry her far beyond her writing assignment. She had a sudden feeling that her visit to Jackson Hole was going to be a journey of self-discovery.

In time, the moose moved away, slowly making its way up an embankment thick with foliage, until finally it disappeared over a ridge. Paige returned to her car and drove on another half mile, where she was able to turn around in a small pullout that served as a parking lot for a canyon trailhead. She started back towards Jackson, passing first the old Manning ranch and then the log cabin that would soon be her temporary home. Seeing the sharp angle of the shadow falling from Dan's barn, she glanced across the valley at the Tetons and realized the sun was rapidly growing lower on the horizon. It was time to return to town before it settled behind the mountains for the night.

Small candles lit up the front windows of the Sweet Mountain Inn as she pulled into the driveway and parked her car. It had been comforting, having the inn as a landing zone for her visit. The innkeepers had been warm and accommodating. Their hospitality had allowed her to feel welcome and their directions around Jackson had allowed her to easily familiarize herself with the town. She would make a point of thanking them when she checked out the next day.

At the small writing desk in her room, Paige pulled out her journal and prepared to jot down some notes. It had been a full day and one filled with intrigue. The land and the people of Jackson Hole were so different from those she was used to back home. The quiet in the air alone was almost a shock. The landscape, the scenery, the culture and the history; all these things were new. Instinctively, Paige knew there was much more waiting to be discovered.

Her thoughts kept returning to the old Manning ranch. An historic ranch could make for interesting reading, especially on the east coast where ranching would be less familiar to readers. But a ranch would have to be unique to the Jackson Hole area in order to be the right subject matter. Some aspect of its history or a tie to a local human interest angle would be needed.

Intuition had often led her to a good story in the past, but she didn't have anything solid to go on this time, at least not yet. Admittedly, a touch of her curiosity was caused by Jake himself. That was something she would have to watch. It wouldn't be the first time a good-looking guy had thrown her off track. Still, she couldn't help but wonder. He seemed amicable enough with people in town, yet he kept to himself. He'd moved into the area recently, buying up a large property that had been on the market for awhile. What was his purpose in moving to Jackson and purchasing that particular property?

Paige sat back in her chair and mulled this over. She needed a reasonable basis for thinking he might be tied into a local story or else she had to focus on the basic article she had originally come to write. So far she had nothing. It would be wiser to start again in the morning and search out other topics of interest in the area.

She lifted her overnight bag from the room's metal luggage rack and placed it on the bed. Grabbing the few articles of clothing that were hanging in the closet, she folded them into a small stack and slid them inside the bag. She left out one pair of faded jeans, a rose-colored T-shirt and a cable-knit burgundy pullover sweater. These would work for quick dressing in the morning. She could already feel a buzz of excitement when she thought about moving to the cabin the next day. But the first thing on the agenda was getting a good night's sleep.

*   *   *   *

Morning arrived with the sound of raindrops pattering on the walkway and tapping against the windows, bringing with it a whistling of wind. Paige peeked out of the curtains of her room at the dark, gray sky and debated the idea of adding one more night at the inn. The idea of staying inside all day, hunkered down in a warm room, was appealing. However, the urge for a hot mug of something caffeinated gave her enough incentive to dress and venture out. She tossed on the clothes she had laid out the night before and twisted her hair up into a loose, haphazard bun. She pulled the hood of her jacket up over her head and broke into a cautious run, watching puddles on the ground and slick sections of wooden boarding that might cause her to slip and fall.

Maddie was behind the counter of the café when Paige walked in, serving a double espresso and blueberry scone to an Italian tourist in line. Old Man Thompson was bent over his coffee at the end of the small counter, just as he had been the last time. Several high school girls were sharing a hot cinnamon roll and sipping chai teas at a round table by the window, repeated episodes of giggles exploding between whispers.

Paige took her place in line, picking up the morning paper while waiting. The front page was dotted with a mix of national and regional news, along with an impressive picture of fighting elk centered just below the Jackson Hole Daily title. The second page held news of the last city council meeting, several small articles about local citizens, an ad for a boot sale and dates and times for upcoming entertainment at local venues. Continuing through the next few pages, Paige found coupons for off-season restaurant specials, classified ads for everything from firewood to hay and a multitude of real estate listings, most of them astonishingly pricey. She was still flipping through the paper when she realized someone was talking to her.

"What can I get for you today," Maddie was saying, likely for the second time, by the look on her face, both patient and slightly annoyed. Paige knew she still had a tourist look about her, something almost beyond definition but clear nonetheless to local residents.

"Oh, I'm so sorry," Paige offered, realizing she'd been lost in the morning paper and not paying attention. "I'll take a vanilla latte and one of those raspberry-orange muffins." She pointed to a basket of fresh bakery items that had just been placed inside a glass display to the right of the counter.

"I noticed you in here the other morning," Maddie said while starting the whirl of the coffee machine. "You must be new to Jackson?" Her voice had an inquisitive, yet friendly tone to it.

"Yes, very new," Paige responded, pulling a few dollar bills out of her purse. "I'm working on an article for a paper back east and came out here to do a little research - historical information, local perspective, that type of thing."

Maddie pushed back the lever on the coffee machine and poured a stream of steaming milk into a thick paper cup, already filled with a shot of espresso.

"Whipped cream?" she asked, with a playful look in her eyes.

"Sounds good, but no thanks," Paige smiled, taking the cup from her and sliding the money across the counter. She leaned to her left and grabbed a plastic lid from a stack of many, pressing it securely against the top of the cup. Reaching back into her purse, she tossed a dollar into a jar marked "Tipping is not just for cows."

"Enjoy your stay," Maddie said casually, her eyes moving to the next customer in line.

Paige thanked her and moved away from the counter, finding a place at a small table in the corner, just behind the front door. She leaned back in her chair, took a sip from the opening in her cup's lid and looked around the room.

The high school girls were just grabbing knapsacks from below their table and tumbling out the front door, accompanied by a flurry of youthful energy and more than a few bursts of laughter. Old Man Thompson was still drinking his coffee, sitting in the same place, bent over his cup in seemingly deep concentration. Either that or he was asleep, Paige thought. It was hard to tell since he never lifted his head, aside from a very occasional sip of coffee. And for that his head was more inclined to move towards the coffee than the other way around. A few tables held local residents browsing the morning paper, while others customers came and went, arriving empty-handed and departing with various steaming drinks and fresh bakery goods in their hands. Outside, the rain continued to fall, tapping against the front windows of the café in a bleak contrast to the buzz of activity inside.

About halfway through her latte, it occurred to Paige that she was glancing at the door each time it opened, observing arriving customers with interest. The sudden realization that she was watching for Jake took her by surprise, as did her disappointment when he did not show. She lingered, reading the paper, finished her latte and muffin and decided to head back to the inn.

Raindrops were still falling as Paige walked the short half block from the café to the main street of town, though by now the downpour had faded into a light drizzle. The gray clouds overhead had lightened a bit, but still hovered above the town. As Paige turned the corner, she noticed the four distinctive arches around the town square that she had seen upon her arrival in Jackson. Sculpted from gathered elk antlers, one stood at each corner of the block that formed the central park area for the town. For a brief second she thought the closest arch reflected a faint light, as if a small ray of sun had slipped through the clouds. Glancing up, however, she saw nothing but the same cloudy gray. Another look back at the arch told Paige she was mistaken about the light. There was nothing but rainy day landscape in front of her. She pulled her jacket tighter and returned to the inn just in time to avoid a crash of thunder and a new downpour.

With the rain continuing to fall outside the window of her room, Paige set about documenting her initial impressions of Jackson. She pulled a small notepad from her suitcase, a spiral bound book with a tan cover. Turning to the first page, she jotted down the general location of the town that had originally been named "Jackson's Hole," after Davey Jackson, an early fur trapper. She described the two main streets, which ran perpendicular to each other in town before veering off in opposite directions. The first, Broadway, headed south, passing through Hoback Junction about ten miles later. It then meandered through the Snake River Canyon and the town of Alpine, finally crossing into the state of Idaho. The other, Cache Street, headed north, passing a multitude of local businesses and many of the town's motels before finally reaching the outskirts of Jackson. Beyond that, it headed through Grand Teton National Park, up through Yellowstone National Park, and eventually into Montana.

It was an amazing place, Jackson Hole. Nothing Paige had heard or read about it did it justice, now that she was seeing it with her own eyes. Set in a bucolic valley and bordered by soaring mountain peaks, it would be impossible not to be impressed by the dramatic vistas the area offered. The most majestic stretch of mountains was the range known as the Grand Tetons, created by shifting layers of volcanic ground and then sculpted by frozen, knife-like glaciers. Surrounding ranges each offered a variety of terrain, trails and landscape. A gaze in any direction would reveal a masterpiece of natural scenery.

Mountain peaks were not the only lure for visitors. Crystal blue lakes were scattered throughout the area, some easily accessible by car and others hidden away, only to be reached by way of challenging trails. The abundant wildlife - elk, moose, bears, wolves and bison, among others – had clearly picked a suitable area for their native habitat. Foliage and berries were abundant during spring and summer months and the backcountry allowed isolation from humans.

Winters were a different story. Harsh weather, sub-zero temperatures and heavy snowfall kept most of the national park areas closed while roads remained unplowed. Though snowmobiles carried adventure-seekers into some of the more distant terrain, ski slopes closer to town were the main draw during these tougher months.

Paige paused for a minute, looked out the window as the rain continued to fall. She thought about the Blue Sky Café and the Sweet Mountain Inn, both appealing as individual, non-chain businesses. There were other unique establishments in town, as well, like the Million Dollar Cowboy Bar, a popular hangout for locals and tourists alike, known for its bar stools made of saddles. Eateries included pizza parlors, steak and game houses and upscale sushi bars, as well as many offering Chinese, Italian or Thai cuisine. Though a town of the old west, it had clearly learned how to artfully feed its residents and to cater to the palates of modern day tourists.

Paige closed her eyes and tried to imagine what the town must have been like years ago, in the late 19th century, when settlers arrived and homesteaded, began trades and started the development of what would become such a popular destination many years later. She could almost hear the rustling of skirts as women walked along the wooden sidewalks. She could imagine the clattering of hooves from horses trotting through town, some carrying newcomers looking to settle, others bringing mail or supplies. She tried to imagine the buzz of conversation that must have taken place on the very streets she had been walking herself the last few days. It would have been an entirely different scene than the one she was witnessing now.

Returning to the paper and pen before her, she sketched out these new impressions. Putting away her notes, she reached into a black, leather case which was leaning against the writing table, pulled out a small, compact laptop, gathered her thoughts and began to compose an email to her editor.

To: Susan Shaw
From: Paige Mackenzie

Re: Article on Jackson Hole

Hi Susan,
*   I've arrived in Jackson, which is turning out to be the most fascinating place. I can't get over how different it is here. The people are wonderful and the entire town is quaint and peaceful.*

Aside from the massive tourism, that is. Thanks for sending me after the summer rush was over!

I've been staying at an inn not far from the center of town, a place called the Sweet Mountain Inn. I've had a small room, nothing fancy, but everything I've needed for these first few days. Being able to walk to most everything in town has come in handy.

As it turns out, I stumbled into a small cabin not too far north of town, on the land of a local resident who makes log furniture. He offered it to me for a very reasonable rate, based on a weekly rental. I think it'll be a good place to absorb the area and begin to set it down on paper. I'll move over there tomorrow, at least for this week.

I haven't started drafting the article yet, but am taking notes and recording initial impressions. I'll be able to start putting these thoughts and details together a few days from now, which will give me plenty of time to get it finished before the deadline.

I'll touch base with you soon, to let you know my progress.

Say hi to everyone in the office.

Paige

Clicking on the "send" icon, Paige shot off the email, turned off and snapped shut the laptop and placed it back in its case. She still preferred to jot down notes by hand, but modern times required modern means of communication and she knew Susan needed a quick update. She was thankful for the convenience of wireless access at the inn and knew she'd miss that once she moved up to the cabin. With the email to Susan sent off, she could now set work aside and get organized.

The rain appeared to be easing. The sound of a steady downpour had given way to a light pattering. Outside, raindrops fell from the edge of the roof, cascading from rain gutters, splashing against the cement sidewalk and disappearing into small puddles. The gray sky had lightened up a bit, though it was far from being sunny. Paige was already learning that Wyoming weather couldn't be predicted. It could be sunny one moment and raining the next. The locals often quoted the old expression, "If you don't like the weather, just wait ten minutes." She was finding this to be true.

She grabbed the overnight bag, gathered her other belongings and loaded up the trunk of her car. Checking briefly to be sure she hadn't overlooked anything, she closed the door behind her. Turning her room key in at the office, she thanked the innkeepers for their hospitality and returned to her car. The sooner she could get into her new living space and start focusing on writing, the better.

She pictured the cabin in her mind as she drove south a mile to the local K-Mart. The cabin had electricity and running water, a small bathroom, but no kitchen. There was a long table she remembered seeing outside, which she hoped to move inside and use for a makeshift kitchen. With this in mind, she found an open space halfway towards the back of the parking lot and headed inside the store, aiming first for the section with home appliances. She wouldn't buy anything that she didn't really need, or couldn't take with her when she left, but she'd buy what she needed to get by in the cabin without too much discomfort.

It was going to be too chilly in the evenings to get by on cold food alone, so she looked over the selection of smaller cooking devices and picked out a single electric burner, which could easily be set on the long table and plugged into the outlet on the cabin wall. She found a can opener in another aisle, making a mental note to pick up a variety of canned soup, dry pasta, a couple jars of marinara sauce and some oatmeal for cold mornings.

She paused in front of a compact microwave oven, but decided she'd be able to make do with the burner and a small sauce pan, which she found on another nearby aisle. Moving on to an assortment of dishware, she was glad to see plates, bowls and silverware stacked and priced as single items. She picked up one of each, adding a ceramic mug with an image of a moose on it. It was all she would need. Having company over was not on her list of plans.

Passing by the bedding section, she was thankful for the sleeping bag she carried with her whenever she was on a road assignment. Rolled up in the trunk, tucked against the side of the car, this was what she'd use to sleep in, saving her the expense of sheets and blankets. She picked up one pillow, to make her nights a little more comfortable. Moving on to a section of linens, she chose a bath towel in a soothing, sea foam green, as well as a hand towel and washcloth to match. She had everything else she needed for the bath with her already.

Taking her selections to the front cashier, she made her purchases and exited the store. She threw the bags in the trunk of her car and headed next to the local market, where she picked up an assortment of food items that would not require refrigeration. It would be easy enough to fix simple meals without using perishables. She made sure to toss some fresh fruit into her basket, an added measure to keep from living on canned and packaged food alone. She could pick up milk or other items as needed, in small quantities. Bottled water would work for a beverage, along with coffee. Again, she was thankful for the items she always carried with her on the road, which included a small coffee maker and a grinder for coffee beans. Thinking of this, she added a package of French Roast coffee beans to her other selections. Impulsively, she grabbed a mixed cluster of fresh cut freesia and iris, along with a few small votive candles, to make the cabin feel a little more like home. She checked out at a front register and added the new purchases to the growing inventory in the trunk of her car.

The drive back through town was an easy one. Even with a few mid day tourists cruising along, the traffic seemed almost nonexistent to Paige, being used to the frenzied pace of New York City. She made a left turn at the intersection of Broadway and Cache streets and headed in the direction of the cabin. Before long, the road passed into the wide, open space that bordered the north side of town. The rain had now let up completely and bright rays of light cascaded down from between the remaining clouds. Appaloosas grazed in a field to her left, gathered in by long stretches of wooden fencing that allowed the horses a generous space to roam.

Twenty minutes later she arrived at the small cabin, pulled her car up alongside the porch and popped open the trunk. There was no sign of Dan and the workshop appeared to be closed. As she approached the front door of the cabin, she found a note tucked into the door jamb.

"Gone to Idaho Falls for supplies. Make yourself at home. Back late tonight, Dan."

Paige looked around at the deserted property, realizing how quiet it suddenly seemed. The noises at the inn had been second nature to her, being so minor compared to the sound level of Manhattan. The street traffic had simply been soft background noise. Late guest arrivals in nearby rooms had gone unnoticed. Yet the absence of sound around her now was almost deafening.

The door to the cabin creaked as she pushed it open and reached for the light switch. A ceiling light flickered on as she stepped inside, casting a weak glow across the front room. She made a note to pick up a small reading lamp the next time she went into town. It was unlikely the cabin's dim light would be enough for writing.

She unloaded the trunk of the car and set about arranging her new living accommodations. With some effort and a few hefty grunts, she dragged the table inside and pushed it against the far wall. She stacked her small collection of dishes to the right and set up the electric burner to the left. Up above, she placed the canned and dry food goods on the lower of the two long shelves. It took a little stretching to reach them, but it kept them out of the way.

Searching around the yard outside, she found an old, green jar, halfway embedded in the ground. Bringing it inside, she rinsed the dirt off the smooth, glass surface and arranged the freesia and iris in it, adding a few sprigs of greenery from one of several bushes alongside Dan's barn. She placed the makeshift flower vase on a small, square table in the second room, setting one of the votive candles beside it. She then rolled out her sleeping bag on the narrow bed and fluffed up the pillow she had purchased in town. This would do, she thought, as she sat down and looked around the room. It was rustic and basic, but comfortable. The bed and table, hand-crafted by Dan, were artfully designed in such a way that they blended perfectly with the antique log structure. The cabin had everything she would need. She was struck by how little it took to get by, thinking of the multitude of belongings at home that she had accumulated over the years. Yes, the cabin would do nicely.

With the weather improving after the morning rain, she moved to the doorway and stood for a few minutes, surveying the property. A few old farm tools were propped against a shed about twenty yards away. A long deserted, metal milk can was resting on its side halfway between the cabin and the parking area. She walked out to it and brought it up to a standing position. Then glancing back at the cabin, she moved it closer, thinking it might make a good plant stand beside the front door.

The porch itself, narrow as it was, looked inviting after the errands she had run and the work she had done inside the cabin. Paige pulled a weathered, wooden rocking chair closer to the door, retreated inside and emerged a few minutes later with a book. Settling down into the chair, she opened the book to the spot she'd bookmarked the last time she'd had a chance to read.

It wasn't long before the sound of an approaching vehicle drew her attention toward the road. Certain that it would be Dan, she watched for his old, white van to pull into the driveway. Instead, she was surprised to see a red pick-up truck pass by. A decal of a cowboy riding a horse decorated the back window of the cab, a symbol she had seen frequently since arriving in Wyoming. The windows were slightly tinted and a thick coat of dust covered the exterior of the truck, similar to most vehicles around town. She watched the truck continue on, pausing for a bison crossing the road before disappearing from view.

Returning to her book, she tried to continue reading, but found it difficult to concentrate. Not only were snippets of possible article topics seeping into her mind, but the temperature was dropping with every passing minute. True to the jokes about the weather, clouds were already starting to form again overhead. A chilly breeze was kicking up, weaving its way through the beams on each side of the porch and ruffling the pages of the book she now held firmly in her hands.

Paige looked up at the sky and knew she didn't have long to move back inside before the first raindrops fell. She set her book just inside the door and walked quickly around the side of the cabin, where a pile of split logs rested against the wall, a thick green tarp stretched across the top. Reaching under the tarp, she grabbed the wood, gathering logs into her arms quickly and moving them to the porch. Two armloads would be enough to stock the small fireplace inside and keep it going for awhile. She finished stacking the wood just as the rain began to pour down.

Using one of several local newspapers accumulated over the past few days, she tore out a few pages, crumpled them into small wads and placed them along the bottom of the fireplace. Building on this, she placed small twigs and tree bark above the paper, stacking several of the split logs on top of those. She found a book of matches in one of her bags and lit the paper. Sitting back, she watched the progression of flames as they slowly moved up from the paper to the kindling, finally catching on the larger logs.

It was soothing watching the fire and again she picked up her book and fell into reading. Only when she heard a sharp thud on the porch, followed by a knock, did she set the book down. She jumped up, crossed the room and opened the door, where she found Dan standing, his clothes and hair soaked from the rain.

"I brought you a little something," he said, pointing to a small refrigerator. "I had this in storage and thought you might be able to use it. I've been meaning to put it in here, anyway. Don't need it in the house. Doesn't hold much, but at least you can keep a few things cold."

"Great," Paige responded with surprise. "I'm sure I'll be able to use it. I was planning to live on canned food and fruit. Thanks for thinking of me."

Dan shook his head in amusement as he lifted the small, square refrigerator and brought it inside, placing it against the far wall, under the shelves.

"I see you've gotten settled in a bit," Dan said, looking around. "Looks nice and cozy, the way it should be." His view took in the glowing fire and he nodded his head in approval.

"I really like this cabin and appreciate your offer to let me stay. Oh, speaking of which," Paige added quickly, turning away and crossing the room. She grabbed her purse off the long table, pulling out the first week's rent and handing it to Dan. He took the money, folded it in half and put it in the back pocket of his jeans, thanked Paige and left, sprinting across the open lot to get out of the rain.

The weather whipped up into a frenzied pace during the afternoon and evening. Paige stayed inside listening to the howling of the wind and pounding of the rain. The sounds of the storm echoed inside the old cabin, creating an isolated feeling and a sense of a larger force. To these haunting sounds of nature, Paige warmed a bowl of soup and ate in front of the fireplace, watching the flames slowly die down. Eventually her eyelids grew heavy and she curled up in the sleeping bag, fluffing her pillow before resting her head and falling asleep.

The storm had eased by morning. Paige made a pot of freshly ground French Roast, poured some into her moose mug and looked out the front window. A light mist covered the mountains, weaving its way between trees. Dan's black lab played alongside the driveway, chasing chipmunks and jumping in and out of low brush. Paige could hear the caw of a crow nearby and turned to see it sitting on the roof of the barn.

Without Internet access, she knew she would have to head into town. It was likely that Susan had returned her email from the day before and she'd need to send a reply. She pulled on faded blue jeans and a red, long-sleeved, button-down shirt, adding a V-neck sweater over that, a dark blue knit with a heavy weave, one of her favorites. She lifted a hooded jacket off a wall hook, just in case the weather took another turn, grabbed her laptop case and cell phone and left the cabin to head toward Jackson.

She pulled out of the driveway and started toward town, reaching up out of habit to adjust her rear view mirror. Looking behind her, she noticed the outline of a red truck, far enough behind her that she had not seen it while entering the road. She lifted her foot off the accelerator to allow the truck to move a little closer, curious if it might be the same one she had seen pass by the day before. Continuing to slow down, she finally pulled over at a scenic turnout, quickly grabbing a map in order to appear occupied. As the vehicle approached and prepared to pass her, she cautiously turned her head to the left, just in time to catch a glimpse of the driver. Somehow she was not at all surprised to find that the driver was Jake.

She waited before pulling back out on the road, long enough to not call attention to herself, but not so long as to lose sight of the truck. Following it into town, she watched it pull into a parking space near the town square. Again she stopped her car and watched as Jake got out of the truck and walked to a bench in the center section of the square. He paced back and forth nervously, glancing occasionally at his watch.

Paige estimated ten minutes passed while Jake paced, during which time his patience appeared to grow thinner, if she read the changing manner of his stride correctly. His steps became uneven and nervous. His arms crossed and uncrossed repeatedly. It was clear he was waiting for something and not at all pleased that it was taking as long as it was. Finally a man approached from the opposite side of the square, dressed in bulky clothing and wearing a cowboy hat pulled forward and to the side. The bench was partially blocked by trees and she was too far away to see their faces, but she could still tell the two men were engaged in a heated conversation. At one point the man who had approached Jake reached into his pocket and pulled something out, handing it over to Jake, who stuffed it quickly inside his jacket. Both men lingered, their arm motions telling Paige that they were speaking a few final, terse words. Finally they parted, moving away in opposite directions.

Watching Jake walk east from the square, Paige suspected he was aiming for the Blue Sky Café and soon found she was right. He crossed through the park, walked under the antler arch and headed across the street, disappearing around the corner. Paige put her plans to check email on hold, locked her car and followed.

The café was packed, more so than it had been on other mornings. Most tables were occupied and a line stretched from the counter halfway back to the door. This allowed Paige to enter un-noticed. She took a place behind the other customers waiting and looked nonchalantly down the line.

Jake was just stepping up to the counter, ordering his usual black coffee. Looking around at the crowded cafe, he took stock of the few available tables and grabbed one in the back corner, set away from the rest. Leaning back against the wall, he quickly glanced around and took the envelope out of his jacket, opening it discreetly and pulling out a folded note. In Paige's judgment, he appeared entirely consumed, his eyes scanning the paper from side to side, at times leaning closer to squint at whatever it contained.

After a few minutes, he folded up the paper abruptly, stuffed it back in his jacket and quickly walked out the door, leaving his coffee untouched on the table.

Paige took her latte to go, opting not to follow Jake anymore. For one thing, he had disappeared too quickly when he hurried out of the café and Paige wasn't sure which direction he had taken. For another thing, she needed to check her email and it had to be done before she headed back out of town.

Ten minutes later she pushed open the glass doors of the library and headed to the computer area. To her relief, there was only a short wait in line. She was soon settled into a chair in front of an empty terminal, logging into her email account. As she expected, there was a response waiting from Susan.

To: Paige Mackenzie
From: Susan Shaw

Re: Jackson Hole Article

Hi Paige,
    Great to hear from you!
    It sounds like Jackson Hole is as interesting as you expected. Glad you are settling in and starting on research.

A couple things to think about:
    Try, if you can, to push beyond the regular tourist information, beyond the advertised spotlights of the area. We

want to find something different, something unusual. We want to give readers an inside view. See if you can get to know some of the locals and maybe some of the old timers, too. They'll know things that wouldn't be readily available through normal research channels.

Also, if you can do as much historical research as you can, it will cut down on the fact-checking we need to do later on.

We have a little time on this one, but I'd like to see it ready for print in two weeks. See what you can do and let me know if you have any problems.

Susan

Paige clicked on the return icon and quickly typed a short response, aware that others were in line for use of the computers.

To: Susan Shaw
From: Paige Mackenzie

Re: Jackson Hole Article

Hi Susan,
Thanks for the advice and direction. I think two weeks will be fine. I've already run into a few locals and will see what I can learn from them. I'll also do some research at the Historical Society, where I can get accurate dates and names of events and people involved with Jackson Hole's history.

Again, thank you for your help and support. I'll give you an update later in the week.

Paige

Paige logged off and stood up, moving away from the computer in order to let the next person in line step up. Heading toward the exit, she rounded a corner quickly, without looking up. A clatter of books slamming against the floor followed her clumsy crash into another library patron. Embarrassed, Paige mumbled an apology while bending down to pick up the spilled books. Two more hands reached down to help, accompanied by a light laugh. To her surprise, she looked up to see Jake.

"Oh my, gosh," Paige stammered, more shocked and surprised to see Jake than she was apologetic for the collision. "I'm so sorry." She scrambled to grab a few more books from the floor and noticed they had titles about Jackson Hole. Some appeared to be history, others maps and trail information. She heard the light laugh again and straightened up to face Jake straight on.

"I really am sorry," Paige repeated, glancing at the books in her hands before looking up. "It looks like you're doing some research on this area. Local books?" She watched for a reaction.

"Jake Norris," he said, shifting the books he was holding to one arm and extending his right hand toward Paige.

"Paige Mackenzie," she countered. She met his hand with her own, feeling a sudden, unexpected shiver at the touch of his skin against hers.

"These books?" Jake said lightly. "No particular reason for them. I just enjoy reading." Still, he clung tightly to the books in his arms.

Paige noticed the edge of the envelope sticking out of the pocket of his flannel shirt. In fact, she noticed the shirt itself, a light blue with gray and white lines in the design. She also noticed his jeans, his rugged skin and the tilt of his mouth, still posed in a slight smile. And she noticed his eyes, a blue-gray that matched perfectly with the shirt. And then she noticed that he was noticing her notice. She abruptly regained her composure, apologizing once more for not watching where she was going. With a thin grasp of dignity, she quickly added that it was nice meeting him. Turning to leave, she could feel his eyes and smile lingering on her back as she walked away.

Feeling oddly unsettled, she stopped to pick up a few more grocery items for the fridge that Dan had been kind enough to provide. With another stop, she added a few utensils and some small pads of paper for taking quick notes. From there she drove into the center of town, making the usual left turn required to head north. The gray clouds had lightened considerably and there was still plenty of daylight left. Impulsively, she pulled the car over in front of the town square.

Paige walked slowly around the perimeter of the park and then crossed diagonally along one of the slatted wood walkways that crisscrossed the square. Clusters of violet primrose and bright yellow dahlia surrounded a tall statue in the center, a memorial to war heroes. She headed toward the bench where she had seen Jake's animated conversation with the other man earlier that morning. Sitting down, she took a slow look around the square. She ran through the scene in her memory, knowing she had been watching from too far away to be sure of any details. But it had been clear that Jake had seemed especially agitated and the man he met hadn't been any less upset. The exchange of the envelope had been done quickly and discreetly, but not before an argument of some sort. After that there had been little or no conversation. Jake had merely tucked the envelope away quickly and walked off toward the Blue Sky Café.

Again Paige ran through the encounter in her mind, wondering what the envelope contained. It had to be important, both because of the way the interchange happened and because of Jake's hasty exit from the café after reading the envelope's contents. Her instinct told her she was onto something and should follow through with it. After all, Susan had encouraged her to pay attention to the local people, to try to get information that was not readily available to anyone who simply passed through town for a day. Whatever was going on with Jake and the other man, it was definitely something outside of ordinary town activity. She was determined to find out what it was.

From her location on the bench, Paige had a view of most of the square. She surveyed the area and paused, taking note again of the four antler arches, in particular the one on the corner closest to the Blue Sky Café. Again it seemed to have a faint glow across the top, just as it had when she passed by it the other day. Looking around at the other three arches, she didn't see the same lighting. She looked up and searched for parted clouds and rays of sunshine, wondering if one might be directed at that particular arch. But there was nothing from above to cause that type of effect. Nor were there streetlights on, which ruled out yet another possible explanation.

She stood and took a few steps in one direction, watching the arch closely as she passed it by, but could see no change in its appearance. Reversing direction, she walked back, but the glow remained the same. Finally, facing the arch directly, she wondered if this could simply be a trick of Wyoming mountain lighting, some type of optical illusion caused by the high altitude. A scientific explanation was starting to sound like something she would welcome.

She approached the arch, expecting to see the light fade, but instead it seemed to grow brighter. Though it appeared to go unnoticed by other people passing by, it seemed clear enough to Paige. Stopping a few yards in front of the arch, she stared at its hazy glow for a few seconds, certain that she wasn't imagining it. She looked around for bystanders who might be able to confirm what she saw, but the town square was now surprisingly empty. When she looked back at the arch again, the glow had completely disappeared.

CHAPTER TWO

The sun was starting to lower on the horizon when Jake pulled up to the fenced gate of the ranch. He stopped his truck just far enough back from the gate to allow it to open, pulled on the emergency brake and left the engine running as he jumped out. The latch was old and rusty and the hinge creaked abrasively into the still air. He made a mental note to replace it at some point. But that would have to wait, along with dozens of other tasks. He had much bigger things on his mind.

He swung the gate open, returned to the truck and drove it through, stopped again and jumped out to pull the gate shut and then continued on to the old farmhouse. He liked the building, old and run down as it was. It had two stories, a small attic and a large front porch that wrapped around the sides. The interior was spacious and boasted an impressive vaulted ceiling above the main room. Yet those features didn't interest him as much as the view across the valley to the Tetons. This was the reason he had bought the property, that and the fact it dated back to the late 1800's. It had cost him an arm and a leg, but he was certain it would pay off in time.

Upon entering the farmhouse, he tossed aside his hat, a typical cowboy style with a wide brim. It was a clean shot, landing on a wooden hook on the wall to the right of the entrance. He dropped his jacket on the sofa and walked to the kitchen, opened the refrigerator and grabbed a bottle of Moose Drool. Savoring the questionably-named but satisfying malty brew, he sat down at the kitchen table and pulled out the envelope.

Damn that Frank, he muttered under his breath. He didn't appreciate being blackmailed and that was exactly what Frank had done, as far as he was concerned. It should have been an easy exchange in the town square that day. Instead it became a dispute. Well, he wasn't going to worry about it now. He had what he'd waited for right in his hands. Now he just had to put the pieces together. After all these years of waiting and searching, of keeping secrets and being cautious, he could feel the anticipation of reaching his long-time goal.

He opened the crumpled paper and stared at it, just as he had that morning in the café. Good old Maddie, he thought, always ready with his black coffee. It was a good town, a nice place to live. It probably would have been worth moving to it anyway, even without a motive. But that was beside the point. He was here now, with business to take care of, not to sit and ponder the benefits of life in Jackson Hole.

The paper in front of him was worn and yellowed, with a rough tear along the left side and a stain of some sort just to the right of the center of the page. Lines, both solid and dotted, meandered across the sheet of paper, crossing at times and staying parallel at others. At one point of intersection there was a mark off to the side, which appeared to be something of a cross between a star and an "x". There was no indication of direction, no typical markings to show north, south, east and west. And there weren't any words on the page at all to give even a general location. An uneven zigzag line wound its way across the upper left side of the page, disappearing into the torn edge. Three symbols resembling arrows were clustered to the right.

Jake set the paper down on the table, took another swig of his beer, and let out a frustrated sigh. This wasn't going to be enough, he thought. Maybe he needed to start over from the beginning, to think it all through again. He felt a sudden, familiar flutter of apprehension, one that he shook off as quickly as it took hold of him. He hated these moments when doubt weaseled its way into his thought process. Hesitation was counter-productive. He brushed it aside and tried to put his thoughts in order.

It was an old legend, though not a familiar one to many, much to his advantage. It was never widely publicized. Few articles had been written about it and those that had been were less than convincing. The lack of evidence was to blame, at least in Jake's opinion. People tended to want something concrete before they would accept a tale as feasible. They sought specific clues or multiple accounts of the same story. The little that Jake knew he'd learned from his grandfather, an eccentric old man with a seemingly wild imagination. Little he said had carried much credibility. He'd told numerous tales during his lifetime, all met with skepticism at best.

But his story of buried loot had captured Jake's attention as a young boy. As he grew up he became more and more convinced that his grandfather's story had some truth to it. It made sense, wild as it sounded, that there could be a stash of treasure hidden somewhere in or around the valley. There were plenty of other legends he'd heard over the years. Some told of stagecoaches that had been robbed, while others claimed various pioneers had found gold and run off with it. Still others described local Native American tribes who had accumulated valuable goods by trade over the years and hidden them away. Yet it had always been his grandfather's tale that he had believed the most.

Jake folded up the paper and carried it into the large living room. He looked around, weighing his options, and then walked over to a tall, oak bookshelf and pulled out a book about Wyoming history. Opening it to a page in the middle, he inserted the map, taking care not to damage the paper any more than it already was. He then pressed the book shut, replacing it on the shelf.

Jake took a moment to survey his book collection. He had just about everything that had ever been published about the history of the old west, in particular those books concerning the area of Jackson Hole. Whatever recent additions had come into print he'd picked up at the library that afternoon, along with any publications about the area's topographical profile or books containing trail maps of the mountains.

He was sure the mountains were the key. Grabbing one of the trail guides, he settled into a comfortable, wing-backed chair, switched on a small floor lamp and began to browse through the book. There were so many possibilities. This was where the hard part came in. In coming to Jackson and purchasing the old Manning ranch, he'd felt he would have a better chance at finding the location of the legendary treasure. Instead, he'd only run into frustration. The valley was too long, too wide, to make this an easy task. Just the trails alone roamed over fifteen hundred miles, all put together. And there was nothing to say the treasure was buried anywhere near a trail. After all, many of those trails had been developed over recent decades. They wouldn't have existed one hundred years ago.

One possibility, Jake had thought, was a trail that looped up past Taggart and Bradley lakes, located about fifteen miles north of town. Another he had considered was an area behind Emma Matilda and Two Ocean Lakes. This area seemed less likely to him, in that it was approximately thirty miles north of town. Still, whoever hid the treasure may have felt more secure keeping it at a distance.

The area that had intrigued Jake the most, though, was up against the Grand Tetons, behind Jenny Lake. Here the possible hiding places were almost endless, as the trail wound up through Cascade Canyon and branched off at a fork, leading in one direction to Lake Solitude and in another to Hurricane Pass. Just to arrive at Hurricane Pass was over eleven miles one-way, not to mention the elevation gain of 3500 feet. Taking the other fork involved a distance of about nine miles total to get to Lake Solitude, with an elevation gain of about 2300 feet. And this didn't include any searches he'd need to do off the trails themselves.

Jake thumbed through the trail guide a little more, looking over other options. Static Peak, accessible through Death Canyon, was another possibility. Nor had he ruled out Delta Lake, reached by trail out of Lupine Meadows. The truth was that it was a huge mountain range with a seemingly infinite number of possible hiding places. Finding the correct one would be a monumental task. But it was not an impossible dream, Jake told himself. He was determined to see it through. He owed it to his grandfather, as well as to himself.

He placed the trail guide by the front door, alongside a pair of well-worn hiking boots. A quick glance around confirmed other ready supplies – a bright flashlight, a small compass and a warm, but lightweight, jacket. It would be easy later on to grab everything quickly and head out to begin exploring some of the trails. At least he could work on ruling a few out. The more he was able to narrow down the search, the closer he'd be to his goal.

Crossing the room, he pulled out the book that held the crumpled map and sat back down in the chair. There had to be something he had missed the first time he looked at it, some other marking or a line that was more obvious than he thought. Turning the three-way light up to its brightest level, he held the map up and peered through the paper. With the exception of the smudged spot just to the right of the center, there didn't seem to be anything hidden. He squinted, attempting to see through the spot, but it was heavily stained and the light did nothing to reveal anything that might be underneath.

The sound of a sudden crash outside brought Jake immediately to his feet. He switched the light off quickly and stuffed the map under the cushion of the chair, then crossed quietly to a front window, pressing his back against the wall to the side of the window sill. He waited to hear more sound, not moving, his heart pounding inside his chest. It didn't seem possible that anyone could know why he was here, what he was searching for. But it made sense to be cautious anyway.

When several minutes passed without any additional sound, he pulled the edge of his front curtains aside and peered outside. Only then did he realize that the sun was almost down, leaving behind only the partial view that was typical for the twilight hour. He hadn't been aware that it had grown so late while he was wrapped up in reading the map and trail guide.

Seeing nothing unusual outside, he moved to the doorway and cautiously opened it. A soft breeze flowed through the opening and the wild grass outside bent with the rise and fall of the wind. There was nothing out of the ordinary that he could see. His truck rested right where he had parked it. The chairs on the front porch were undisturbed. Everything seemed to be in its proper place.

Jake closed the door, twisting the lock a little more attentively than he usually did. Without turning the lights back on, he made a circle of the house, checking latches and briefly looking out of each window. Still he found nothing unusual. The sound must have been an animal running through the property, he decided. It was not uncommon.

To calm his nerves, he returned to the main room and opened a tall, oak cabinet. He pulled out a round glass snifter and a decanter of brandy, setting it on the small table beside his chair. He poured a generous serving and settled back, taking a gulp, followed by a few smaller sips. The warmth of the sweet liqueur spread down his throat and into his chest. He took several deep breaths and finally found himself relaxing. It had been nothing, he figured. Just the normal sounds of the open range, the regular noises to expect when living in this territory.

CHAPTER THREE

It was still light when Paige returned to her cabin, even after making additional stops to run errands along the way. At the post office, she had dropped off a handful of postcards to friends back east. In the local thrift store, she had browsed around for a few more items.

She parked her car in front of the cabin, unloading a reading lamp and a large, oval, braided rug that she had found at the thrift store. Taking these inside, she made a second trip to her car for a small bag of groceries, which she took inside and put away. She set fresh fruit and banana nut muffins on the table, next to the coffee pot. This would cover breakfast the following morning.

While it was still light, Paige brought in an armful of firewood and stacked it to the left of the fireplace, where it would be ready for use later on in the evening. She pulled a chair up to the small writing table and pulled out her laptop. It was time to start outlining her notes so far, transferring them from the small notepad where she had been jotting down brief tidbits over the last few days.

Jackson Hole – Notes

Jackson Hole is named after fur trapper David E. Jackson, an early partner in the Rocky Mountain Fur Company. Originally named Jackson's Hole, referring to the entire valley as a "hole," it was later changed to simply Jackson Hole.

Pre-1800 – Area was used by Native Americans for hunting and fishing. Tribes included Shoshone, Nez Perce, Crow, Blackfeet and others.

1803 – Lewis and Clark expedition organized by Thomas Jefferson. Expedition reports helped inspire westward movement.

1806-1808 – John Colter, a member of the Lewis and Clark group, traveled into Jackson Hole to scout for fur trading.

1845 – Fur trapping declined as styles changed. Other means of earning income were developed, including the opening of early dude ranches, aimed at bringing visitors in to enjoy the area's hiking, fishing, hunting and scenery.

1862 – The Homestead Act allowed settlers to claim land for the price of making improvements. Many settlers arrived, both American and European. Early settlers included John Holland and John and Millie Carnes.

1871-1878 – The Hayden Surveys officially named many landmarks, including Jenny Lake and Leigh Lake.

1872 – Yellowstone, just north of Jackson Hole, became the world's first national park.

1888 - Population of the valley was 20 men, 2 women and 1 child.

1889 – The first Mormons migrated to Jackson Hole.

1890 – Wyoming became a state.

1892 – Population of Jackson Hole had grown to 60 people.

1892 – The first post office was at Marysville, which closed when the Jackson Post Office was opened in 1894.

1894 – Town of Jackson named.

1897 – The Jackson Hole Gun Club built The Clubhouse, which was the first community building.

1897 – President Grover Cleveland set aside the Teton Forest Reserve.

1899 – Deloney's General Merchandise was the first store to open in Jackson.

1900 – First Jackson Hole census. Approximately 600 people living in the area. Five post offices existed in the valley.

1901 – Hotel belonging to Mary Anderson, which had been located at Antelope Gap, was moved to the Jackson town site, becoming the Jackson Hotel.

1901 – Bill Simpson laid out plans for the town of Jackson, using typical grid format common for the time.

1903-1905 – The first local school was located in The Clubhouse, and then moved to a log building.

1906 – Roy Van Vleck and brother Frank arrived in town and started building a cabin, later opened as Jackson Mercantile.

1907 – William Trester's first photo of town. Tuttle and Lloyd's Saloon already visible.

1908 – President Theodore Roosevelt established the Teton National Forest.

1909 – First edition of Jackson Hole Courier published. Population now 1500.

1912 – U.S. Biological Survey Elk Refuge was established.

1914 – Town of Jackson incorporated.

1920 – Jackson elected the nation's first all-female town council.

1921 – Electricity powered Jackson for the first time.

Pre-1924 – Town square was just a depression covered with sagebrush.

1924 – Town started to improve the square by bringing in dirt to fill it.

1931 – Town brought in plants and landscaping.

1941 – Roads around the square were paved, cutting down dust problems.

Paige hit the save button and shut the laptop down, waiting for the lights on it to click off before slowly closing the top. She'd learned quite a bit about the area since arriving in town, but it was clear that there was much more to learn. It wasn't as easy as just talking to the locals, though that had been good advice from Susan. She needed to get beyond that, to get to the information that even the locals didn't have, or didn't know they had.

She had always been one to trust her instincts. It had worked for her on other articles, such as the famous pirate Blackbeard's hidden cove on Ocracoke Island, or the quiet life of the Kentucky Shakers near Harrodsburg, Kentucky. Sometimes it was worth following a hunch more than just facts. But usually the real payoff came in following both, in finding whatever way the two could weave together and create something not otherwise visible. It was one of the challenges of writing, combining research and imagination. She loved searching for the magic point where the two intersected.

Standing up, she left the small desk area and moved to a front window. The sun was almost gone; only the faded images of twilight remained. She could hear the wind rustle through small patches of sagebrush outside. The screen door creaked a little as the breeze washed through the front porch. There was some sort of mystery in the air. It wasn't anything she could put her finger on and it wasn't anything that could be found in any of the research she had done. But it was there, nonetheless. This was the part that intrigued her the most, the instinctual part. She had a hunch that this time it was the factor that would pay off. All she had to do was find the right combination, the right key. She had a feeling somehow that Jake would lead to this. She just had to find out how.

Impulsively, she grabbed a jacket and stepped outside. If following instincts was what she had to do, then that was exactly what she would do. She eased her car out of the dusty driveway and turned out on the road, heading in the direction of Jake's ranch.

Other than a few bison grazing by the side of the road, dark shadows against the twilight sky, she found the road deserted. This wasn't a surprise to her. She'd learned quickly after arriving in Jackson that the activity was mostly centered in town, much of it directly around the town square itself. It was only necessary to drive a few miles in any direction to reach some solitude.

As she continued along, she spotted a faint light in the direction of Jake's ranch. It twinkled in the semi-darkness like a star that had decided to appear on stage a little early. It grew slightly brighter as she approached, but there appeared to be only one window that glowed. She surmised it couldn't be much more than one small light. Perhaps he wasn't even home.

To play it safe, Paige parked her car on the side of the road, finding an area that was slightly lower than the roadside fence, allowing her car to stay out of view of the ranch. She proceeded on foot another hundred yards or so, until she came to a point along the wood post and barbed wire fence that allowed her to see the old farmhouse clearly. With quiet steps, she approached the fence, bent down a little and peered through.

A bald eagle soared across the sky, landing on the higher branches of a tree that was about halfway between Paige and the house. A lone coyote roamed the fields to the east, prancing about and lunging at small rodents and other animals who were about to become supper for the clever hunter.

Paige eased her way along the fence until she arrived at a point where there was substantial brush on the other side, large enough clusters to hide behind. There, without giving a second thought to fact that she was trespassing, she slid carefully between two of the fence's wires. She moved from one cluster of sagebrush to the next, crouching down to avoid being seen, until she found herself in a location where she had a good view of the house.

Still only one window held light. The glow was brighter than it had appeared from down the road and it cast a small area of light out onto the front porch of the farmhouse. Inside the window she could see the outline of a man's head from the side, with the face tilted slightly down. He appeared to be sitting in a chair of some sort, something with a high back. The light was set behind him, preventing any illumination of his features. Seeing the familiar red truck parked alongside the house, though, Paige knew it had to be Jake.

She watched the silhouette of his head move back and forth, turning slightly from side to side. Perhaps he was just stretching his neck, she thought. Or he might be working with his hands, maybe whittling some wood or repairing an appliance. Or maybe he was reading, Paige suddenly thought, remembering all the books he'd been holding at the library earlier that day. It occurred to her at that moment that he might be researching the area, just as she was. Maybe he'd come to Jackson Hole for more than just the real estate investment of the old Manning Ranch. As Dan had mentioned, Jake had family ties to the area going back generations.

She watched as he rose up, moved away from the window and then returned again, holding something in his hand. Another book, Paige guessed as he took a seat again in the chair. He must be looking for something in these books, she thought, watching him reach up to adjust the light. What was it? Was it hidden in the past history of the area? Was it something concerning Jackson as a town right now? Whatever it was, it had to be intriguing, as he remained in the same spot for some time.

Paige moved forward, still staying a good twenty yards or so from the house. She inched behind another cluster of sagebrush, this one fairly thick and wide. The outdoor light continued to fade as night approached and the view inside Jake's window grew even clearer. She remained crouched down, peering above the sage brush only slightly. It was at this time that she felt the presence of someone or something nearby.

Turning slightly to her left, she suddenly gasped, seeing the coyote that had been running loose on the side of the property standing not ten feet away. Holding her breath, she watched him as he watched her in return, a quiet stand-off in silence. He took a step closer, which caused Paige to gasp again. She waved her hand quickly, as if to whoosh him away by suggestion, but this had no effect. The coyote continued to face her, staring at her with small, puzzled eyes. Finally Paige picked up a small rock from the ground and, in desperation, pitched it at the animal, though not hard enough to cause sizable injury. She hoped only to scare it away.

It worked, but not in the way she might have hoped. The coyote jumped back at the sight of the incoming rock, brushing against some shrubbery and then bounding off in the direction of the house. Paige watched with a terrified, sinking feeling inside her as the coyote raced around the corner of the front porch, crashing into a stack of old crates sitting just to the side of the house and causing them to fall over. It then veered off into the fields and disappeared into the distance.

Her heart pounding, Paige stayed motionless behind the large cluster of brush. There was no sound from the house, but she could see the light inside quickly extinguish itself. In the growing darkness, she felt frightened and vulnerable. After all, she didn't belong there. She was clearly trespassing and she didn't even have a decent excuse to give for doing so. She didn't even have one to give herself.

Paige remained frozen in place, hearing nothing but silence for a few minutes. Then, at the creak of the front door opening, she took advantage of the slight sound to flatten herself down on the ground, where she knew she couldn't possibly be seen. She held her breath and waited for what seemed like forever, until she finally heard the door latch shut. Still, she remained on the ground, the smell of dust in her nose and the scratching of dry brush against her clothing.

Eventually she eased herself up off the ground and, remaining crouched down, moved cautiously from sagebrush to sagebrush until she found her way back to the opening in the fence. She slipped back through it and quietly but quickly hurried down the road to her car. Her hand shook as she inserted the key into the ignition, but after a couple false, nervous tries, she got the engine running and pulled out onto the road, making a hasty retreat to her cabin. Here she parked the car along the far side of the building, rather than out in the general parking area, and then slipped inside the front door, Latching it shut, she sat motionless until dark had fallen completely.

CHAPTER FOUR

Jake paced back and forth across the town square, frustrated and angry. How stupid could he be, believing Frank the way he had? He was as much of a liar as his grandfather probably was, raising him on all those ridiculous stories of buried treasure. His grandfather had pulled the wool over his eyes and now so had Frank. He should have seen it before, but that only made him as stupid as the others.

Pausing to lean against the monument in the center of the square, he pulled a pack of cigarettes out of his pocket, tapped it against his hand, pulled one out and pressed it between his lips. With his right hand he patted his chest and then his hips before finding a book of matches, somewhat torn and wrinkled from being carried around in his pocket, but useful nonetheless. He coughed a little on the first puff, just a reminder that he had quit smoking years ago. But extreme times called for extreme measures. He was just about at the end of his rope.

Jake shifted his weight from one hip to the other, then leaned back casually again. It wouldn't help to appear nervous, he thought. It was a good thing he calmed down and settled back, because when Frank came walking up, he wasn't in any kind of a calm mood himself.

"What the hell do you think you're doing, calling me out here like some little servant?" Frank was fuming and he wasn't about to hide it.

"I need more information from you," Jake stated calmly, looking Frank directly in the eye.

"I already gave you everything I have," Frank insisted, though the look in his eyes told Jake otherwise.

"Listen up, now," Jake said, the calm tone in his voice and manner starting to quickly slip away. "I didn't spend all this time, all these years and all of this last particular year getting to this point, only to have it all ruined by you." He pointed his finger at Frank for emphasis, then dropped it and looked around to make sure they weren't attracting attention by causing a scene.

Jake lowered his voice and moved his face closer to Frank's. Even without words, the communication was clear. Frank now shifted his weight back and forth, considering the unspoken statements.

"I want the rest of the information now," Jake said slowly. "Don't even try to tell me that paper is everything you have. I know better. For one thing, the tear on the side of the paper hardly looks a hundred years old. And the smudge doesn't look that old, either, now that I think about it." Jake ran an image of the small map through his mind.

A woman walked by, accompanied by a small terrier on a leash and a young girl, who she pulled in closer to her as she passed the two men. Frank and Jake waited until they were alone again before continuing.

"OK," Frank said carefully, keeping an eye on Jake while he spoke. "I might have something else for you, but..." His voice trailed off and he looked at Jake inquisitively.

Jake threw back his head and laughed, then brought his gaze directly into Frank's eyes. "Don't even think about blackmailing me for any more money. You've gotten all that you were promised. Now it's your turn to hold up your end of the deal." His eyes didn't waver until Frank started to nod his head.

Frank looked around nervously; making sure no one else was approaching.

"Here's what we'll do," he said, lowering his voice as a precaution. "We're not going to meet in this place again. Too many times will look suspicious. For all we know, someone could have already seen us and wondered what was going on." Frank paused and looked around again, then stopped with his gaze on Cache Street, directly across from the town square.

"I'll meet you tomorrow night at the Million Dollar Cowboy Bar. It's crowded there and we won't appear obvious to anyone. Besides, a good, tall lager sounds pretty good to me." Frank shrugged his shoulders and stretched his neck to one side, then to the other.

"Well, at least that's one thing we agree on," Jake answered, imagining a cold beer in his hands right then. "You're on, but don't let me down on this one. I already told you I held up my side of this deal. Now you're going to follow through."

With that the two men parted ways, Frank heading toward one antler arch and Jake heading toward another. It would be a long twenty-four hours, Jake thought to himself, but he'd make use of the time. And tomorrow night he'd have his answer.

CHAPTER FIVE

Paige took the narrow, dirt road east, climbing out of the flat land and winding into the hills. Tall rows of aspens lined the road, sunlight filtering through the last remaining leaves of gold and orange which represented the tail end of fall foliage. The sunlight cast sharp angles low across the ground, almost horizontal in the rapidly setting sun. Beyond a rocky scenic overlook, the road swung sharply down in switchbacks before flattening out beside a lake. Signs marked the way to a campground, spaces inside empty and quiet. Yet an open gate, not yet locked for the coming winter, allowed Paige to turn in.

She followed the driveway towards an area designated for a boat ramp, turning left just before it and parking near a small picnic area, which looked out over the water. The surface of the lake was rippling and a chilly breeze hit her face as she stepped out of her car. Paige followed a path to a picnic table, took a seat and stuffed her hands in her pockets to try to keep them warm.

The sun was just slipping behind the horizon and wisps of clouds had started turning from a pale, whitish-yellow to a soft, light pink. An echo of the same pink settled over the lake, illuminating the ripples across the water. As the daylight continued to fade, the pink clouds turned to a deep rose and finally to nothing more than dark gray. The outline of the mountains became pronounced, appearing as jagged edges against the remaining sky.

A few cows called out from the other side of the lake, distant silhouettes along the shore. As the light faded even further, one lone tree stood out in front of the water's edge, its barren limbs reaching up into the sky. The thin, stark branches stood out in dramatic contrast to the warmth of the sunshine that had just departed.

Paige shivered and pulled her jacket tighter around her, watching the final acts of the evening's sunset performance. Even as the mountains started to fade into black, a shimmer of light remained on the water, a mirror of the sky. Like an inseparable pair, they would continue to fade away in equal measure until the blackness of the mountains reached out and took hold of the space above and below. Soon the cows would blend in with the hillside, the lake itself would become one with the shore. Dark green pine trees would meld together into one picture of night without anything to distinguish one part from another.

Once again Paige felt the lure of the area. Tall mountains, so dramatically sculpted they were almost unbelievable, a town with the sense of history and hidden secrets, and now this awe-inspiring sunset over the lake. Paige knew she'd fallen into something unique and unusual. There were many shades to the magic of Jackson Hole. The rosy hues of the evening sunset were just parts of the total spell. When the dark had almost settled in completely and the chill became too much to bear, she returned to her car and headed back to the cabin.

Dan was working by kerosene lantern outside the barn when Paige pulled into the driveway, hammering a golden colored lodgepole branch into a flat sheet of burl to form one corner's leg. Three more legs of similar shape, size and length rested against the side of the barn. He stopped hammering and called a greeting over to Paige, who responded with a wave as she continued walking to the cabin. The hammering started up again as she stepped inside and closed the door.

Again she sat before her laptop, recording the observations of the day. She looked over the history notes she had already made, trying again to get a sense of what the town had been like in its early years. She tried to imagine the early settlers, how hard it must have been for them to come into the valley and even survive, much less make a home for themselves. The winters were frightfully difficult. There was no electricity in the late 1800's, when people first arrived. The wildlife, although beautiful, could also be dangerous. It was certain that some succumbed to attacks from wild animals who acted to protect their young or to guard sources of food. And then there was the lawlessness, the drinking and carousing that undoubtedly caused additional problems. Gunfights and territorial arguments must have taken many to their graves, as well.

Paige shut the laptop and built a fire, warmed a cup of soup and curled up on the braided rug, which she had placed a short distance from the fireplace. She let her thoughts run at random, thinking of the soothing sunset over the lake and continuing to contemplate the scenes that must have played out in the days of the old west. When she felt sleep descending, just as the dark had fallen over the lake, she pulled a pillow off the bed and fell asleep with the warmth of the fire on her face.

CHAPTER SIX

The sun was nowhere to be found when Jake sat up and stretched the following morning. Looking out his window he saw only heavy mist covering the mountains and a white layer resembling soft cotton stretching out below. Only the tip of the peak known as The Grand stuck out above the foggy scene, awe-inspiring in its stance 13,770 feet above sea level.

Jake pulled on jeans and a faded sweatshirt and headed to the kitchen to make a pot of fresh coffee. Over the first few sips of the rich brew, he watched a sliver of lightning streak down from the sky, followed by a sharp crackle of thunder above. He fixed a bowl of corn flakes, sprinkling far too much sugar on top, a habit he knew he needed to break. From the kitchen window he watched the rain begin to pour down, slamming against the ground with sudden fury. More thunder and lightning followed, to his dismay. He would need to wait the weather out before heading off. Another delay, he acknowledged reluctantly, just what he didn't need.

He moved into the main room, setting the cereal and coffee on a rectangular pine table in front of the couch. Walking by habit to the bookcase, he pulled out the hidden map. He sat back in the comfortable, wing-backed chair and studied the map in a little more depth. Tracing his fingers along the tear in the left side, he looked at the zigzag line again, which followed the left margin of the page, small segments occasionally disappearing off the side, as if the line had originally extended beyond the tear. It must be the mountains, he thought. Nothing else would have that shape. The treasure must be on the other side, on the section of the map he was now convinced Frank would bring him that night. This fit with his theory about Cascade Canyon, which extended deep enough inside the mountains to be located on the portion of the map he considered missing. Perhaps the zigzag line indicated a direction, not the mountains themselves. Or it could be both, for that matter. There was no way to know without the missing piece.

Once again he held the smudged section up to the light, twisting the paper in different directions to see if anything showed through. There was nothing he could see, just as there hadn't been when he looked before. It would be a long day, waiting for the meeting that night with Frank. Resigned to a rainy morning, he closed his eyes, map clutched in his hand. He tipped his head to rest against the back of the chair and waited.

CHAPTER SEVEN

The rain was slick on the pavement as Paige drove into town. It didn't matter, she knew she had to fight through the storm and get to the library to email Susan. It had been several days since they had corresponded and it was time to give her an update. If only she knew exactly what to say.

A few locals were scattered around the library when she entered, either slouched in chairs reading, or working at small tables. One library worker pushed a metal cart stacked with books, scanning shelves as she moved down the aisles and stopping occasionally to insert a book here or there.

Paige was relieved once again to see the computer area wasn't crowded. A teenage girl occupied one seat and an older woman with bifocals leaned in toward a monitor not far from where the teen sat. Paige took a place near the corner, glad to find a computer available that had some privacy. She logged on and opened her email to compose a letter.

To: Susan Shaw
From: Paige Mackenzie

Re: Jackson Hole Article

Susan,

It's quite the rainy day here in Jackson Hole. We've had thunder and lightning since the early hours. I stayed inside for much of the morning, to avoid the slick roads, but then made my way into town to touch base with you.

I've done some research this week on the history of the area. It's a fascinating place, settled by homesteaders in the late 1800's with more arriving as the century turned. Life was extremely hard for the early residents of this community. From a historical aspect, it's possible an article on this would be of interest to history buffs. I'm not sure how marketable that would be, but it's one of the possibilities.

On the other hand, I think I may have stumbled onto something on the local level, though I'm still trying to figure out just what it is. There are a couple locals here who've been meeting in the town square, exchanging envelopes and that sort of thing. One has also been doing research on the area, which I know from bumping into him at the library. Literally, that is, but that's another story altogether. It's just a hunch, but I have a strong feeling there's something behind all this.

I'm going back to the town square today, even if the rain continues. There's something unusual going on and I think I should pursue it.

I'll get in touch with you again in a couple days. Maybe I'll have something concrete for you at that time. I'll keep trying.

Paige

Before leaving the computer, Paige pulled up Google and ran a search on Jackson Hole. Getting too many hits, she narrowed the search by making her query more specific, first by running the words "Jackson Hole History" and then "Jackson Hole Early Settlers." From there she followed links to several websites, jotting down notes as she found bits and pieces of information. She ran a check for bibliographies on the research results she found, printing out several lists of book titles. Logging off, she gathered the printed pages and headed for the aisle on local history.

Following the numbered signs on the ends of the aisles, she wasn't surprised to find that the section she was looking for was right around the corner from where she had bumped into Jake. She moved down the middle of two tall rows of books, scanning the titles as she went along. Pulling a few volumes off the shelves, she found a comfortable chair where she could browse through various chapters.

The first two books were very general, recounting tales of grizzly bear encounters, difficulty getting supplies into the valley without direct train lines, and sawmill development to help with logging for early settlers. But it was the third book that caught her attention, a slender bound text with a dark blue cover. The chapters were brief and were spread over a range of topics, from homesteading history to wildlife conservation to the gradual acquisition of land that would eventually become Grand Teton National Park. As she skimmed through a few chapters, one subject in particular caused her to pause.

Among the many people who had come to Jackson Hole around the turn of the century were prospectors. These men had come into the valley following rumors of gold. Many of the searches centered along the Snake River, which wound its way through the valley from north to south. Following a winding path, the river had provided many opportunities for panning gold. The mountains, on the other hand, had allowed many opportunities for hiding it. Though the accounts in the printed volumes stated that no substantial amount of gold had ever been found, Paige couldn't help but wonder if this was true. The written records showed such small amounts of gold accumulated, it almost seemed impossible that there wasn't more. After all, it didn't say there wasn't any gold in the valley, only that very little had been discovered. What if there had been more gold discovered than history books showed? Perhaps there were discoveries that had gone unreported. It wasn't beyond reason that lucky prospectors might have kept the more lucrative finds a secret.

Paige approached the front counter of the library. A slender young woman with braided red hair and dangling silver and jade earrings walked over to the counter, asking if she could help.

"What does it take to obtain a library card?" Paige asked.

"Just some identification and an address," the woman answered, reaching for an application form as she spoke. "A phone number is good, too."

Paige paused and thought for a moment. She didn't have a local address, but had her cell number. And she might have an address at the cabin, but hadn't a clue what it might be. She did, of course, have a driver's license, so there was some form of ID she could provide. Giving over this information seemed to be enough. Within a few minutes she had her driver's license number, cell phone, and a general delivery address gathered together. She soon left the counter with a library card in hand.

She returned to the chair and the bookshelf, selected the slender, blue book, along with several others on general area history. Additionally, she picked out a few trail guides, hoping they might give her some possibilities of locations where gold might be hidden, providing her hunch was correct. It was a long shot, she figured, but it was worth following. Hidden gold would certainly make a story of interest to the paper's readers back in New York.

Gathering the selections into her arms, she approached the library's check-out desk, catching the attention of the library clerk and speaking up in a voice that would not disturb others in the room.

"Excuse me," she whispered across the counter to the clerk. "Are there any more books about the history of gold prospecting in the area?" It couldn't hurt to ask. There could be books that had been returned, but not yet placed on the shelves.

The clerk's earrings swayed as she shook her head from side to side, jade and silver catching slivers of light from the bulbs hanging from the library ceiling.

"I'm sorry," she replied apologetically. "We usually have more on that subject, but they were all checked out recently. Would you like me to notify you when they become available again?"

"No, that's ok," Paige answered as casually as she could. "These will be fine for now."

She checked out the books she'd already chosen, stashing them in an empty tote bag in the back of her car. It was still raining, though it had let up a little. A steaming latte sounded good. She headed over to the Blue Sky Café and found a parking place directly across the street.

Maddie was behind the counter, as always. Old Man Thompson was hunched over his coffee in his usual spot, a buttered bagel resting on a small plate next to the coffee cup, though it appeared to be sitting untouched.

There were a few customers, but not the usual line, most likely a result of the rain. Had she not needed to go into town to use the library computer, she probably would have stayed home herself.

Maddie greeted her with recognition this time and it occurred to Paige that she had already become a regular. At least she had certainly frequented the Blue Sky Café often enough to have it appear that way.

"How's it going, local girl?" Maddie said teasingly. "Last I heard you were just visiting, doing an article on the area. No pressing deadline, I take it." Maddie took Paige's order and moved to the coffee machine, starting up a whirling of steamy noises.

"Oh, it's just such an interesting area," she told the café owner lightly, watching her pour frothy milk into a heavy paper cup. "I decided a little more historical background would make whatever I write more interesting. I found some good resources at the library. They have a great section on local history." She demonstrated this by indicating the stack of books in her tote bag.

"You're right about that," Maddie said, taking Paige's outstretched payment for her latte. "There's certainly an interesting history here in this valley, no question about it."

Paige thanked her and moved to a comfortable spot to read, the back corner where she'd seen Jake sit before. With the café as empty as it was this morning, she had her choice of places to sit. The one she chose was a small booth, as opposed to one of the wooden tables. For one person it was quite spacious. She placed her drink on the table and the tote bag on the bench beside her. Pulling out the blue book, she took a sip of her latte and thumbed through the pages, finding the section that had intrigued her at the library.

According to historical accounts, Walter W. Delacy set out with a group of prospectors, starting first in Montana and then working their way down through Jackson Hole. They followed the Snake River south, covering the valley and then passing through what was now known as Hoback Junction, searching along the portion of the river that ran through Snake River Canyon. Flanked by cottonwoods, they moved along the limestone terrain, eventually running into sandstone toward the end of the canyon. Doubling back, they searched the valley again, camping along the Gros Ventre River and then moving north to Cottonwood Creek and Pacific Creek. At Pilgrim Creek they set up a mine along the river, but gave up when their work went unrewarded.

Paige paused to look around the room while her mind circled this information. Were their efforts really unrewarded? History was not always accurate. Once again her instincts told her there was something beyond the basic account in this book.

She noticed Maddie had caught up with customers and was wiping down countertops. No one remained in the café except for Old Man Thompson, who, as always, remained hunched over his coffee. She watched him take a small sip before setting it down once again. Her gaze returned to Maddie and she decided to approach the counter. It couldn't hurt to try to get a little more local information. That had been what Susan suggested and it was good advice. Not all answers could be found in printed material.

"Hey, Maddie," Paige inquired. "You've lived here awhile, haven't you?"

Maddie laughed and shook her head with amusement. "All my life, honey. And my mother before that. And her mother before that. Each statement was spoken with more emphasis than the one before.

"I had a feeling," Paige replied. "So I'm wondering if you might know any local legends. You know, the kind that might not be in the history books, but have been passed down from generation to generation." Paige waited while Maddie appeared to think this over.

"What kind of legends are you looking for?" Maddie questioned in return. "This is a small town. Small towns always have legends. Some are true and some are not, but they're always floating around."

"Well," Paige began hopefully, "I'm particularly interested in the old stories of the prospectors who came through this area, what they might have found or not found during their explorations and mining attempts." She waited for Maddie's response, watching her turn away to wipe down the back counter. When she turned back, she had an expression on her face that was a cross between blank and puzzled, as if she were thinking the question over carefully.

"I doubt I'm going to be able to help you on that one," Maddie answered. "That's one subject I don't know too much about, other than what we learned in school. But I'm sure that matches whatever you've read. The way they came into the valley, searched around and didn't find much of anything. I think the lucky ones were the ones who went on to California and other areas. The guys who stayed here kind of got short changed."

Paige sighed and nodded her head. "That's what I figured," she said, thanking Maddie for the information. She noticed Maddie scrubbing the coffee machine vigorously, perhaps trying to remove splashes of espresso from the morning's business, turning next to the task of stacking ceramic mugs on the back counter. Paige returned to her corner booth, gathered together her books, replaced them in the tote bag and, waving goodbye, stepped out of the café onto the sidewalk.

Pausing a few steps from the door to rummage through her purse for car keys, she heard the clanking sound of the cups stop and recognized Maddie's voice speak up. With no other customers in the café, her comments could only have been directed at Old Man Thompson.

"I don't like this," Maddie said quietly. "I've got a bad feeling about it." Paige waited to hear a response from Old Man Thompson, but he remained silent. Finally she heard the thud of a fist hitting the counter.

"Don't worry about it, Maddie," a gruff voice responded. "She's just passing through." He spoke with an annoyed tone of confidence. "You worry just as much as your Aunt Ruby did and she drove everyone crazy. Besides, this girl's reading those history books and there's nothing about this in there. She ain't gonna find nothing here."

"I hope you're right," Maddie's voice replied. As the conversation ended and the stacking of mugs resumed, Paige crossed the road, heading in the direction of her car.

CHAPTER EIGHT

Jake spent the morning listening to the rain pounding down on his roof. He spent most of the afternoon pouring over the maps he had accumulated over the years. Worn and faded, yet not nearly in as bad a shape as the paper Frank had given him, these were the maps he had analyzed as a child, comparing the visual layout of the land with the stories his grandfather told him. Now he pulled the reading light a little closer and looked carefully at the Jenny Lake area and the section of mountains directly behind it.

From the south, the area could be accessed by following the trail up through Lupine Meadows and then skirting around the south end of Jenny Lake. From the north, a trail from the smaller String Lake wound its way around the north end of Jenny Lake, making this an alternate route. In modern times, Jake knew, a boat was available to whisk visitors across the lake, thereby shortening the hike into Cascade Canyon. At the time the nineteenth century turned to the twentieth, however, hikers would have had to take one of the other routes.

Once they arrived on the west side of the lake, they would need to start their ascent, arriving before long at Hidden Falls and, just beyond that, at Inspiration Point. Ruling out the boat crossing, this was approximately a three mile trip. Though not a difficult hike in current times, reaching Inspiration Point would have been more difficult in the early 1900's, as the present, steep trail was not cut through the granite rock until the 1930's, when the task was accomplished by the Civilian Conservation Corps.

Another three and a half miles would take hikers to the Forks of Cascade Canyon, where there was a choice to branch off in a northward direction toward Lake Solitude or to head south toward Hurricane Pass. Jake was betting on Hurricane Pass as the most likely, just because of the remote location. It wouldn't have been an easy hike for the early settlers, but it was probably far enough from the more frequently traveled valley to let them feel safe about hiding their stash.

Jake continued inspecting the maps for a good part of the afternoon, then folded and set them aside. He took a long, hot shower and prepared for his trip into town. Reaching into his closet, he pulled out a white shirt and his best pair of denim blue jeans. He followed this by selecting a tan, leather vest and a shiny belt buckle with the shape of a buffalo sculpted into the metal. Checking his appearance in the mirror, he ran his fingers through his hair, still wet from the shower. Tossing it around a bit, he decided it could dry on its own.

The Million Dollar Cowboy Bar wasn't terribly crowded when he arrived, but by the looks of the busy sidewalks, Jake knew it would be filling up soon. The regular doorman, Billy, tipped his cowboy hat at Jake and waved him in.

"How you doin', Mr. Norris?" Billy asked as Jake flashed a grin his direction.

"Doin' fine, Billy, doin' just fine," Jake answered, taking a quick look around the room.

"What brings you out on a cold night like this?" Billy asked, more for small talk than anything else.

Jake glanced over his shoulder to respond as he sauntered by. "Just hangin' out, figured a beer or two might taste good." Billy nodded in agreement before turning back to the door to check the ID's of a couple young ladies. Jake continued on into the room, passing a row of pool tables before arriving at the well-known bar counter. Swinging his leg over a saddle, he nodded a hello to the bartender.

"Hey, Deke," Jake called out, "How about a cold one?"

The bartender gave a thumbs-up sign in Jake's direction and opened the door to a refrigerator under the counter. Pulling out a tall, frosted glass, he angled it under one of the spouts for draft beer and filled it most of the way, then turned it upright at the last minute, allowing a perfect head of foam to settle on the top. He placed it in front of Jake and slapped his hand playfully against the bar.

"One Snake River Lager, Jake, old boy. That'll be three bucks for you."

Jake pulled out a billfold from the back of his jeans, leaning to the side a bit in order to reach it. He slipped out a five and slid it across the bar. "Keep the change, Deke. It's always a pleasure doing business with you."

Taking a slow drink of the amber liquid, he looked around the bar and took in the usual nightly scene. A few men stood casually around one pool table, leaning on cue sticks and watching one man take a shot. In the far corner of the bar, a band twanged out a country song, spotlights casting a red glow on the stage as the musicians played. A few old timers danced on the wooden floor in front of the band. Several men in jeans, boots and cowboy hats leaned against the far wall, eyeing the room and watching for any attractive ladies who might show up.

There was no sign of Frank. Jake kept an eye on the door, forcing himself to look around only occasionally, so as not to appear too anxious. He began to feel irritated at having to wait. Frank had inconvenienced him enough. He'd had just about all he was willing to take, and then some.

The band broke into a run of old classics – Merle Haggard, Johnny Cash, Waylon Jennings and Willie Nelson. Jake was tapping his foot to a rendition of "I Walk the Line" when he saw Frank enter the bar, glance casually around the room and then walk over to where Jake sat. He took a saddle next to him and told Deke to serve up one of whatever Jake was drinking.

"How're you doing tonight, Jake?" Frank said with feigned politeness, handing Deke exact change for his beer.

Jake waited until Deke walked away, knowing that bartenders often heard a little too much of everything said at the counter.

"Don't mess with me, Frank," Jake said, lowering his voice. "I'm all out of patience with you. Don't even think about wasting any more of my time."

Frank paused a few seconds, just on general principle, and then reached into his pocket, pulling out an envelope that looked much like the first one he had passed to Jake in the town square.

"I don't know if I should even trust you," Jake mumbled with exasperation. "How do I know this one will be different from the other?"

Frank stood up, gulped down the rest of his beer and looked Jake straight in the eyes. "You'll see," he said. "Put the pieces together and you'll be on the right track. You probably could have done it with what I gave you before, but maybe this will make it easier for you." He dropped fifty cents on the counter as a tip for the bartender and then turned toward the door and left, stepping aside only briefly to let a few people enter the quickly filling venue.

CHAPTER NINE

Paige hoisted her tote bag over her shoulder and walked to her car. She opened the door, tossed the bag across to the passenger seat and then straightened up to look at the sky. The rain had stopped, at least temporarily. But she had gotten to know Jackson Hole too well by now to trust the weather to stay the same for very long. Still, it was nice to have a break in the rainfall. The gray clouds were slightly lighter in color, though there were no patches of blue sky to be seen. She looked up the street toward Snow King, the pine covered mountain that bordered Jackson, rising to an impressive altitude of 7780 feet. A layer of fog hovered across its slopes. A glance in the other direction brought her gaze upon the town square, deserted at the moment.

Paige paused, narrowing her eyes a bit. It seemed once again that there was a slight glow coming from the antler arch. She looked up at the sky, as was now her habit, to check for a ray of sun that might be slipping through the clouds anywhere, but there was nothing. She pressed the lock on her car door, pushed it shut and walked briskly toward the arch. It seemed ridiculous to be irritated by an inanimate object, but enough was enough. If it was some sort of prank, she intended to get to the bottom of it.

As opposed to the other times she had seen the mysterious light surrounding the top of the arch, this time it didn't fade away as she approached. Instead, it appeared to deepen, blending mysteriously with the misty air. She stepped closer, stopping when she was just a few feet away. Looking around, she saw the square and sidewalks were still deserted.

She took a few more steps forward, continuing until she stood almost directly underneath the well-known, stacked antler landmark. Above her, the glow continued to grow even brighter. Paige was certain this time that she wasn't imagining it. The light quickly grew diffused as it spread outward into the air, but the immediate glow on the arch itself remained constant.

Paige looked around for some sort of logical source for the light, perhaps an electrical plug for Christmas lights that had been turned on early. But there were no power outlets or cords anywhere and she saw nothing else out of the ordinary. The antlers simply rose from their cement bases with nothing attached in any way.

Once again Paige looked around on the ground surrounding the front of the arch and then focused her attention on the walkway. What appeared to be an old, rusty skeleton key rested at an angle on the ground, just a few feet beyond the arch. She looked around, thinking she might see someone who had dropped the key, but there was no one on the square or surrounding sidewalks. Curiosity finally getting the best of her, she stepped through the arch and reached for the key.

* * * *

Paige picked the key up in her hand, feeling the coarse texture of the rust against her skin. Aware of a sudden sensation of tightness around her chest and some difficulty breathing, she straightened up, unprepared for the scene that met her eyes.

The well-maintained landscaping and central statue of the town square were nowhere to be seen. There was no neon sign across the way announcing The Million Dollar Cowboy Bar and not a single souvenir-stuffed shop in any direction. Nothing but dust stretched out before her, a concave hollow of dirt mixed with a few stray bushes of sagebrush scattered across the land.

Bringing her hand to her chest, she found the source of her shortness of breath wasn't only the shock of the change in scenery, but the stiff undergarment of a corset, tightly laced beneath a soft, red satin bodice, trimmed with antique ivory lace. A full skirt of matching fabric flowed down from a tight, pleated waistline. The hem rested mid-calf, just above a pair of dressy black boots with tassels dangling from their upper edges. Several layers of colorful petticoats peeked out from below the hem of her skirt.

Paige felt a shiver of fear run up her spine and crossed her arms in an attempt to fight off nervous shaking. She struggled against the restrictive corset to take deeps breaths and bent forward to rest her hands on her knees. Whatever was happening to her, panic would not help the situation.

Straightening up, she looked around and shook her head in disbelief. Perhaps there had been some sort of drug mixed in with her latte. It all seemed so real, not at all like the haziness of a dream. As if to affirm this feeling, a clatter of horse hooves approached on the left. Paige watched as a weathered wagon passed by, haphazardly loaded down with supplies – barrels of vegetables, an old stove pipe, a couple of bales of hay and other assorted goods.

She glanced cautiously around, noting very few buildings. Those that caught her eye were weathered and rustic in nature. A store of some sort stood across the open grounds, bearing a sign across the top that announced it as "Deloney's General Mercantile." There were large gaps between the buildings, simple, open spaces of dirt. The scene resembled a ghost town movie set, so sparse were the surroundings. Still, other commercial establishments lined the dusty streets – the Jackson Hotel and a pitched roof structure called The Clubhouse. A handful of smaller businesses were also scattered about, offering services of varying trades.

Paige moved hesitantly across the open space and, still struggling to breathe, took notice of a few more details. A slight twinge of curiosity began to seep into the continuing feelings of uneasiness and fear. She stepped into Deloney's store and glanced around. A portion of the shop clearly served as a market, offering apples, potatoes, flour, corn starch, syrup and numerous other types of provisions. The remainder of the establishment housed just about every type of household item one could imagine, from sewing supplies to hardware, as well as basic machinery and farming tools.

Back outside, she slowly began to wander through the town - if it could be called such, with only a handful of buildings in sight. Yet, as empty as the landscape appeared, activity surrounded her. Customers emerged from Deloney's store carrying boxes of assorted household goods. A few men leaned against the outside of a blacksmith shop, having an animated conversation that involved a good portion of laughter and knee-slapping. A mother walked by holding a young boy's hand tightly in her own, scolding him for misbehavior. Though sparsely populated, it was clear to Paige that the activities of a town were going on – trade, communication, and various aspects of community life.

Paige paused in front of the building with the sign above the door identifying it as The Clubhouse. Playful sounds of piano music floated out into the dusty air and seemed to beckon her from within. Hoisting her skirt up to avoid tripping, she climbed a handful of stairs to the front door and slowly stepped inside.

The music was upbeat and grew louder as she entered. A few other women stood around, some dressed in similar garb, though the colors and fabrics varied. One neatly coiffed woman with auburn hair and elegant green attire fanned her face with one hand and rested the other on the arm of a rough looking man. Yet another, a slender brunette with sultry eyes, sat in a chair against the wall, her back straight and poised, as if waiting for a cue. The music stopped briefly and immediately started up again with a different tune, this one even livelier than the last. The woman in the green dress was drawn out toward the center of the floor by the man she accompanied, where the two began to dance. Another gentleman crossed the room, grabbing the hand of the brunette, gently pulling her to her feet and escorting her to the dance floor, as well.

It was a festive atmosphere, bustling with music and laughter, but it hardly seemed a place that would help Paige get her bearings. She was just turning to leave when the sharp voice of an older woman called out.

"There you are, little lady," the voice shouted from across the room. Paige glanced over to see the woman bustling rapidly towards her. She was a little heavier than the other women and the lines on her face gave her age away as at least a couple decades down the road, as well. She charged up to

Paige and grabbed her arm, pulling her over to the side of the room.

"Finally," she said with exasperation. "They said they were sending you, but we expected you a few days ago."

"They were sending me…" Paige repeated, her voice trailing off before her words could manage to take on the tone of a question.

"Yes, they were sending you, just not very quickly, if you ask me" the woman muttered, patting Paige's hair with her hands and, holding her by the chin, turning her head to one side, then to the other. "It's just not that easy to get girls out here. This is Jackson, not one of your big towns. Now let's get you a little more painted up. You're not going to please any men with a plain face like that."

"I…" Paige started to object, but found she was essentially speechless. The woman grabbed her hand with an awkward tug and quickly whisked her across the floor.

"Now, Maylene. That's your name isn't it?" The pause that followed lasted only a split second, not long enough for Paige to even respond. "Of course it is, that's who they said they were sending." The woman parked Paige in a chair and patted on some face powder and rouge, followed by eye shadow and red lipstick that must have been as bright as her dress.

"My name's Pearl, but you can just call me Mama. I take care of all you girls. If you've got a question or a problem, you just bring it to me."

Paige was quite sure at this point that she had a whole string of problems, but she wasn't about to spill them to Pearl, who stood above her now in a huffy, matronly manner.

"Now you remember this is a respectable hall. We only employ fine young ladies, not any of those other types.' Pearl pulled back, eyed the newly painted Paige and gave a few clucks of approval. "Your job is to make sure the men have a good time, dancing, drinking and talking if they're in the mood to run their mouths a bit. But at the end of the night they go home. The rest of it ain't your job. Just remember that."

Opening her mouth to try to explain that this must be some kind of a mix up, Paige felt a hand on her left arm and a slight pull away from Pearl. She turned to find herself looking into the face of a decent-looking man, dressed in business-like attire. His clothing was a notch or two upscale from what the men on the street had been wearing.

"So you're the new girl they sent up from Denver," the man stated, with a tone that made it obvious that he was pleased. "Well, you owe me the first dance, then, seein' as I'm the one who brought you up here. It's about time you showed up." He pulled her out to the middle of the floor, alongside the woman in the green dress and her dance partner, both of whom nodded a kind hello.

The man rested one hand on Paige's waist and lifted her hand with the other, keeping a respectable distance between them as they started moving their feet to the music. Paige followed along, instantly grateful for the cotillion classes she had been subjected to as a pre-teen.

"You're a pretty one, you know. We don't always get the best dance hall girls out here in Jackson, but you're as fine as they come." Paige started to say something and, using her better judgment, decided instead to merely smile. It was enough to just take all this in, without having to form any responses. She had a feeling she could get by, for the most part, with a simple smile for awhile, while she tried to figure out what had happened to her.

"As I was saying, we don't get many of the best girls here," the man repeated. "The fine ones usually go on to

California, out to San Francisco where the bigger dance halls are. But this is a fine place here, Jackson is. You're going to be glad you came here instead."

The woman in the green dress, who was just circling by at that moment, nodded her head in agreement. "Glad you're here," she whispered from a few feet away.

Paige wasn't so sure she could agree. At the moment a martini at the top of the San Francisco Hyatt sounded just fine to her. And a first class airline ticket to get there would promise a smoother flight than whatever she'd just taken.

She looked around the room and saw a few more men entering. Most seemed to be fairly respectable types, not like a few of the characters she'd already seen around town. They removed their hats once inside and nodded a few hellos around the room before mingling in with the crowd.

"I see you're lookin' around at your new home," the man remarked. "It's a nice building, this place. It was built by the Jackson Hole Gun Club, back around 1897. And it's not just a dance hall, you know. We call it The Clubhouse. We use it for settlin' our legal disputes and we can gather together and smoke here, too." The man seemed immensely proud of all this. "Of course, bein' a lady and all, you don't smoke, but us men, we love to get together now and then and partake."

Well, I don't smoke anymore, not since quitting a few years ago, Paige thought to herself, but decided it would be wise to not state this out loud.

The music ended and the man escorted her to a seat at the side of the room, thanked her for the dance and promised he'd be back to dance with her again later on. From there he left, joining a group of men by the front door.

The woman in the green dress had parted with her dance partner on the floor and now moved swiftly in to sit beside Paige.

"I am so glad you're here, honey," she said, fluffing her hair with her right hand and pulling her skirt aside in order to take a seat on the chair next to Paige. "We've been wondering for weeks who the new girl was they were sending up here. My name's Susanna, you know, like the song, "Oh, Susanna." She hummed a few bars, and then continued. "And I know you're Maylene, they told us your name before you got here."

What good would it do to try to correct anything at this point, Paige wondered? And even if she wanted to, it would have been impossible to get a word in edgewise. Susanna kept right on going, telling her about the dance hall, the customers, the town, her beau, her other friends, where she lived and where to get the best price on flour.

"You'll just have to see the new dresses in at Deloney's, back in the corner. There's one about your size in the prettiest sapphire blue. It would be beautiful with your dark hair, Maylene. And it's got little pearls around the neckline and at the ends of the sleeves. Oh, and the neckline is low enough, without being too low, if you know what I mean." Susanna turned her head slightly sideways and gave a little wink. Before she could continue on this time, however, both girls were startled by a crash just outside. Following others, they moved over to the front door to take a look.

Three large, wooden barrels rested on their sides in the middle of the dusty road, piles of potatoes spread out across the dirt. A crude wagon was at a standstill, angled slightly in toward the building. Dust rose up from the ground where its wheels had come to rest. Two chickens ran squawking away from the scene. In the center of the commotion an older man stood wearing overalls and a shirt that may have been white at some point in the past. He pulled a tattered hat off his head and threw it down on the ground.

"Dang it, Russell. Why can't you ever watch where that horse of yours is going?" The man stomped on his hat with one foot, then stepped back and kicked it with the other. The hat went flying, landing on a small pile of potatoes a few feet away.

"Stomping that hat of yours into the ground ain't gonna change anything, Zeke," a bystander shouted from across the road. "You know Russell's not the best driver in the west. You just have to watch out for him. Anyway, he's long gone by now." He waved his arm down the road, where the back of another wagon was just retreating in a cloud of dust.

Zeke huffed and turned around in a circle, surveying the damage. "Well, if you ask me, that man shouldn't even be allowed on the road, much less on that horse of his."

Paige watched bystanders shake their heads and go back to whatever they were doing before the commotion. It was obvious that this was a regular occurrence, most likely repeated frequently by the same two characters.

Susanna pulled on Paige's sleeve and motioned for her to come back inside.

"You can't have much pity on those two, Zeke and Russell," she said, laughing. "They're always in some sort of scuffle. It's been going on for years and it'll probably go on for a lot more."

"I take it they're regulars around here," Paige commented, feeling any comment would be better than staying as quiet as she'd been so far.

"Regulars?" Susanna laughed again. "There ain't nothing regular about those two. They're about as irregular as can be. Now you want regular, you take Jeremiah. He's a quiet sort, but ain't nothing else odd about him. Stays out of trouble, keeps his mouth shut. You can always find him hangin' out down at Tuttle's place, but he stays out of fights and other things, gambling and the like. Not like some of the other boys down there."

Paige looked at her inquisitively. "Tuttle's place?" She asked, more for conversation than anything else.

"Yep, Tuttle's place, the saloon," Susanna said. "Don't worry. You'll get to know the town in no time. Tuttle's is the place where you can find out just about anything that goes on in this town. Not a fit place for a lady, though. I'm just warning you. People get the wrong impression about ladies who go in there. Or they get the right one, depending on the case."

Susanna turned to smile at a well-dressed man who had approached while they were talking. Reaching her hand out, she accepted his unspoken invitation to dance. Paige watched the two walk away and then stood and eased her way around the room towards the door, trying to appear casual and not attract attention. When she reached the front of The Clubhouse, she slipped outside.

Most of the potatoes and household goods were loaded back on Zeke's wagon, though he still stood there muttering to himself. Paige passed by quietly and walked down the road, small bits of dust kicking up around the heels of her boots. She passed a couple young boys sitting on the ground, thumbs plunking marbles across a flat section of dirt. A woman walked past with a high necked blouse and street-length skirt, glancing sideways at Paige with a slight frown of disapproval.

She arrived in front of Tuttle's Saloon and stood outside, taking in the building. It was, like the other buildings, built of wood, with a tall, false front. It was a style she was familiar with from watching old westerns and from photographs of old ghost towns. But to see it right in front of her was another story.

The front of the saloon was plain, but had a porch that ran the length of the building, with four tall beams holding up the small, sloped front roof. True to classic western saloon style, there were two swinging doors at the entrance. In spite of Susanna's warning, Paige summoned up her courage and stepped inside.

The bar was long and elegant, carved exquisitely from a wood that appeared to be mahogany. Behind the front counter a tall, wide mirror covered the wall, elaborately decorated with gold designs. The counter itself was sturdy and long with bar stools all along the front. A few men sat at the bar, most wearing hats, white shirts, vests and pants made of heavy cotton fabric. Four other men sat at a table in the corner, cards in their hands, looks of concentration on their faces.

To Paige's immense relief, it wasn't crowded and she didn't seem to attract much attention. A couple of the men at the bar took a look her way, but turned away to nurse their drinks, whether out of more desire for what was in their glasses or out of disapproval at seeing a lady inside the saloon. The men playing cards kept their attention focused on their game, one tapping his foot nervously below the table, another slouching back with a sly smirk on his face.

One man at the end of the bar, sitting alone, caught Paige's attention. He portrayed the classic look of a cowboy, someone well-suited for his western surroundings. Though missing the stereotypical modern-day jeans and boots, he wore a weathered hat, tilted forward. The chestnut brown hair below that was slightly ruffled, as if a gust of wind had just blown across his shoulders. His neck and forearms were deeply tanned. She guessed his age to be around twenty-five, give or take a year or two.

As an excuse to get closer, she approached the bar and asked the bartender for a glass of water. He looked at her as if she were either crazy or lost, but poured her a glass of water anyway, sliding it slowly across the counter. He didn't speak and Paige didn't offer up any conversation, other than a quiet "Thank you." She turned away from the bar and then, feeling suddenly conspicuous, turned back and tried to make herself as invisible as possible.

Hearing the slap of the swinging doors behind her, she threw a quick glance over her shoulder. A man of about thirty years of age had entered, short but stocky in build, with a gruff expression and air of condescension. He looked around and walked over to the man sitting quietly at the end of the bar.

"What'll it be for you today, Cyrus?" The bartender called down the bar, clearly giving the man more of a welcome than Paige had received. She wasn't surprised, having been warned by Susanna that women weren't welcome in the saloon.

"Just the usual, Slim. A glass of your best rotgut barrelhouse whiskey, and the sooner the better." He slapped his hand on the counter, perhaps out of impatience or perhaps for emphasis. "Oh, and give Jeremiah another of whatever he's having, too." He tossed a couple silver dollars onto the counter and turned to Jeremiah and lowered his voice. Paige inched a little closer. Thankfully, the two men didn't seem to notice.

Though Paige couldn't hear all of their conversation, she was able to pick up bits and pieces. Between gulps of whiskey, Cyrus and Jeremiah seemed to be working out a plan, though what it was about Paige couldn't tell. Phrases such as "back at the cabin" and "ain't safe there" and "when I know, you'll know" were fairly clear. The tones of the voices raised and lowered, as if some degree of disagreement existed between them, but nothing they wanted others to notice.

Looking sideways carefully, Paige saw that Jeremiah had not changed positions, eyes focused on his whiskey, which he swirled in circles with a steady movement of his glass. Cyrus, on the other hand, shifted his weight back and forth, fidgeting with his drink and appearing impatient. At one point the conversation remained too hushed to make out any of the words, but seemed to quicken and become animated, voices rising as it did. Cyrus pounded his fist on the counter and leaned in toward Jeremiah in a threatening manner, then pulled back and took a large gulp from his glass.

"You'll just have to trust me on this one," Paige heard one of the two men say. She guessed from the rough tone that it must have been Cyrus. Jeremiah didn't respond, but leaned forward, falling directly into Paige's view. She snapped her head back quickly in an attempt to cover up her eavesdropping.

Cyrus, however, seemed to have noticed her, because he set his glass down on the bar, straightened up and stuck both his thumbs in his belt, one on each side of a large silver buckle. He walked slowly over to her, his boots clicking sharply on the sawdust-covered wood floor.

"Maybe the lady needs a whiskey," he said, tossing the words down the bar to the bartender. Paige began to shake her head, suddenly wishing that she hadn't had the nerve to come in. She pulled up straight, hugging her arms close to her sides, as if this would somehow give her protection. Cyrus moved a little closer and leaned one arm on the bar, his other hand reaching out to touch Paige's hair.

"Leave the lady alone, Cyrus," a voice stated firmly from behind him. Cyrus turned to find Jeremiah facing him squarely, clearly meaning business.

"She's not bothering anyone," Jeremiah said, continuing to stare Cyrus squarely in the face.

"Well, the way I see it, she don't belong in here if she ain't lookin' for trouble," Cyrus said, lifting his shoulders and raising his eyebrows, as if to demonstrate that this was an obvious fact. "This ain't no place for ladies. I figure she must want some kinda trouble if she came in here."

Jeremiah took another step toward Cyrus. "Well, you figure wrong. It's none of your business why she chooses to come in here or not come in here. Now you back away now, Cyrus. I mean it."

Cyrus looked back and forth between Jeremiah and Paige, who stood motionless by the bar, watching the two men. He considered the situation and Jeremiah's insinuations, and decided it wasn't worth taking a chance. He tipped his hat to Paige, just as if he'd never stepped away from his proper manners, turned around and walked across the room and out the door, leaving it to swing behind him.

Paige looked over at Jeremiah and whispered a thank you, still a little shaken by the incident.

"It's no bother," Jeremiah said, regarding her with curiosity before lowering his voice to match her whisper. "But he's got a point, ma'am. As he said, this ain't no place for a lady."

"I guess you're right," Paige agreed, taking the cue to leave before more potential trouble could rise up. "I think I'll just go now. Thank you again."

Jeremiah tipped his hat and went back to his place at the end of the bar, turning his head back only once to watch Paige as she walked out the door.

The road was quiet as she stepped through the swinging saloon doors and out onto the porch. It appeared that Zeke had loaded up most of his spilled goods on his wagon and moved on. Only a few loose potatoes remained scattered around the road. Fearing a lecture back at The Clubhouse if she returned after taking an unexpected break, she headed off down the dusty road, toward a few structures on the outskirts of the newly-forming town.

On what might be considered a side street, there were a few other buildings with tall, western-style false front exteriors, as well as others not much larger than sheds. One appeared to be a blacksmith's shop, while another seemed to provide building supplies and machinery. Others offered various services to the growing community, from taxidermy to dental treatments. Paige winced, imagining what a trip to the latter might entail. In the distance, a church rose up, sturdy red brick giving it a stance of permanence.

Paige paused in front of one building front that had a large piece of machinery in the window. Putting her hand to her forehead, she pressed her face up against the window, attempting to see inside. It appeared to be a printing press, large and clunky, not at all like the sleek machines of modern times. Of course, Paige realized that, to the people she had just met, these were modern times. This particular printing press was likely considered a marvel to this community.

Stepping back, she looked up at the letters painted across the front of the small building. "Jackson's Hole Courier," it announced, triggering a memory from the research that Paige had been doing. Indeed, the valley had been called Jackson's Hole before the name was simplified.

She tried the door, finding it locked, and then scouted around on the ground, where her eyes came to rest on a small paper caught underneath the side of an old barrel. She reached down and gently pulled the paper loose, straightening it out and turning it right side up, so that she could see the print.

Her heart felt a faint flutter when she saw that the date at the top of the page was Sept. 27, 1909. It matched the scenes that had played out in front of her, but the whole scenario still seemed impossible. Though she recalled her step through the glowing arch, the reach for the skeleton key and the instant change of surroundings when she stood back up, it just wasn't feasible.

She scanned the front of the paper and noted several small articles. One announced building plans for new structures around town. Another recounted a dispute over a homesteading tract along the river. Yet another gave information on navigating the pass. Paige could hardly imagine what a trip over Teton Pass would be like in 1909. It was difficult enough getting over the pass in current times, considering the steep grade and often slippery road conditions.

On the second page of the four page publication, Paige's eyes fell on an intriguing article. An expedition had worked its way up along the river, stopping at numerous points to pan for gold. Though it reported that only traces had been found, it seemed to imply that perhaps there was more to the story than the members of the expedition were telling. Realizing it could be pure speculation on the editor's part, or even an attempt to entertain the paper's readership, Paige wasn't sure it could be taken seriously. Still, it seemed to fit in with her growing suspicion that gold had something to do with the mysterious activity she had come across, both in the past and the present. Or was that the future, she wondered, considering where she seemed to be standing at the moment?

Paige read carefully through the article, which told of a difficult trip, rough camping conditions, a few scares with wildlife who didn't appreciate their calm territory being disrupted and a list of names of the men in the expedition. Somehow she was not surprised to find both Cyrus and Jeremiah's names in that list. The account stated that no significant amount of gold had been found, yet also commented that a few of the men weren't talking about the trip, asserting that they didn't have much to say. Paige couldn't help but wonder if some weren't talking because there wasn't much of anything to report, while others weren't talking for other reasons.

She skimmed through the rest of the paper, which consisted of a variety of notices. Some indicated claims filed for homesteading sites, while another advertised new merchandise at Deloney's Store. One small article listed supplies expected to arrive in town the following week, already en route from Denver. There was an account of an unexpected meeting with a few members of the Shoshone tribe, though no problems had resulted from the encounter. Small tidbits about people around town also followed, resembling a modern-day gossip column.

Paige clutched the newspaper and looked around her dress for some place to hide it. There didn't seem to be any pockets and the corset didn't allow so much as air inside, so there certainly wasn't room for paper. Finally, Paige folded it into a small rectangle, pressed it as flat as possible, and stuck it into her left boot, where it rested just below the edge that boasted the black tassels. She could feel the paper scratch against her leg as she walked, but it wouldn't be noticeable from the outside.

Hearing the sound of horse hooves against the ground, Paige turned to see a wagon passing by. There were four passengers riding on benches above the turning wheels and a driver seated on a slightly higher level in front, his hands holding reins attached to two horses. The driver nodded a hello to Paige, continuing on down the road, eventually pulling into a barn of sorts. It wasn't as large as the barns that Paige had seen in the Midwest, but it was large enough for the wagon and entourage to pull inside.

Paige followed, approaching the building and peering in from outside. She found an open space with a high ceiling, a few rays of light pouring through the wood beams and resting against a hay-covered floor. Several horse stalls lined one side of the building. Two wagons, including the one she had seen pass by, were parked against the other side of the building's interior. As the passengers finished stepping out of the wagon, the driver folded up a step ladder that was attached to the side. Securing it with a short length of rope, he turned to the front of the barn, at which point he noticed Paige.

"Are you lookin' for a ride somewhere, little lady?" the man said, brushing a few pieces of hay off his sleeves. He wore a derby type hat in a dark brown shade which seemed to match perfectly with his thick mustache. He was short, at least shorter than Paige was herself, and had a business-like demeanor.

Paige considered the question, in view of the fact she wasn't even sure how she had arrived where she was. It was a little hard to decide, all things considered, how she could explain where she really wanted to go. A journey of one hundred miles might be a stretch, but one hundred years would certainly be out of the question.

Surely this short but agreeable man would need some type of directions, Paige thought, considering her options. The possibilities included returning to either the dance hall activities in The Clubhouse or the clearly anti-female territory of Tuttle's Saloon. Or she could take the risk of ending up somewhere different, which didn't seem any worse of a choice than the others at this point. With this in mind, she looked around and then back to the driver, telling him that she would, indeed, like a ride.

"Well, you've come to the right place, then," the man said, introducing himself as Chester. "I'll just hitch up my smaller wagon and be right there." He disappeared out a back door, leaving Paige to look around a little more.

Old pieces of farm equipment hung on the barn's interior walls and a stack of metal buckets leaned against a side door. A black crow flew in through the front of the barn, circled around a couple of the wood beams, continuing its path of flight down and out through the back door. As it flew out, Chester returned, motioning to Paige that her ride was ready. She followed him out the back, where a small wagon stood ready, hitched up to a brown quarter horse of sturdy build.

"Just climb on up here," Chester said, pointing to a step ladder similar to the one she had seen attached to the larger wagon inside. He reached a hand out to help her step up, which she accepted, climbing the steps awkwardly in the cumbersome dress and taking a seat on a bench inside the wagon.

"Where to, ma'am?" Chester asked as they pulled around the barn and approached the road.

Paige thought for a minute, and then gave the only answer she could.

"I don't know," she said honestly. "I think I'd like to see a little of the countryside. Just go ahead and drive a little ways out of town." She paused a minute before adding, "Somewhere that you like, Chester. That will be just fine."

Chester gave her a puzzled look, clearly used to people asking for rides when they had somewhere specific they needed to go. But he turned the wagon out onto the road anyway, heading south, away from the town, along a dusty stretch. To the left, an impressive mountain of evergreen trees soared skyward, looking very much like the landscape Paige recognized from present times. To the right stood the familiar, small butte that she also recalled, with rolling slopes and a brown covering of low brush.

As they came to the end of the butte, Chester turned to his right and continued on, circling around and eventually taking a narrow road up the west side. It was a bumpy ride and Paige grasped the wagon's side panel more than once for support as she was jolted by the uneven surface of the dirt road. But, at the end, the view paid off. Pulling the wagon to the edge, he brought the horse to a halt. From this vantage point, Paige and Chester looked down on the town together. The outline of the town's beginning was clear, a layout of crossing roads, with buildings scattered along the dusty streets, most separated by empty lots. Behind the town, the mountain that would later be called Snow King stretched across like a backdrop.

"This is my favorite place." Chester said quietly. "This is where I come to do my thinkin'." He sat still, looking out peacefully at the town.

"I can see why," Paige agreed, taking in the wide open land that surrounded the few buildings below.

"It's building up fast now, this little town. Got our own telephone system, the Jackson Valley Telephone Company," Chester added with pride.

"So, you have a telephone?" Paige asked, genuinely excited for him.

Chester threw back his head and let out a laugh the size of the valley itself.

"What in the world would I need one of them modern contraptions for?" He shook his head with amusement. "Everybody knows where to find me." He glanced around, debating other tidbits of information worthy of a little boasting.

"Do most people live here in town?" Paige asked nonchalantly, already knowing the answer, but wanting Chester to get a chance to brag a little more.

"No, ma'am," he replied quickly. "This whole valley's fillin' up with homesteaders. Why, just last year the president of these United States opened up a whole lotta land north of here, up for grabs. Folks started filing claims right quick. Now ranches are springin' up so fast the elk can barely find food these days, all their grazing areas blocked off with buck-rail fences."

"I worry about them animals," he continued. "We got a whole lotta dead elk up there in the valley, seein' as they can't find enough to eat. Some folks in town are workin' on a petition to send to the government, askin' them to set aside an area for the elk to feed. I hope they get it."

Chester paused to consider what he'd just said before adding a few more examples of the town's developing status.

"But, as I was sayin'," Chester continued, picking up the topic of conversation again, "Jackson's Hole is growin' and it's gonna continue to grow, I figure. We've already had a ferry crossing the river for six years, thanks to Bill Menor. And it's been ten years already since Pap Deloney opened his store. We even had one of them new-fangled automobiles come through this year, way north of here, trying to go through Yellowstone. You're a smart lady, it seems, so I'm bettin' you know that's been a national park since 1872.

Anyway, they were fools. I heard they found out them things ain't allowed in the park. Had to take it through on a wagon. No, Tuttle's place wouldn't be hoppin' the way it is if not for all them folks comin' into this valley."

He crossed his arms, clearly satisfied with his portrait of the growing valley.

"Now, look over here," Chester said, motioning for Paige to turn her head to the far left. "Back there behind us a ways we got ourselves a dude ranch, the JY. Just set up operations a couple years ago. People are thinkin' it'll bring visitors in, fetch us all some extra dollars. Sure would help me, more folks needin' to git around."

"I thought most people here were cattle ranchers." Paige watched as Chester nodded his head in agreement. "And others grow oats and barley," she added, trying silently to run through her recent research of Jackson Hole, but coming up short with specific chronology.

"Well, now, they do that," Chester agreed, nodding his head. "They grow alfalfa and clover, too, even some wheat. But it's not enough for most people to get by. And there's lots to see around these parts, things more folks ought to see. So they're hoping visitors will come."

"I have a hunch they will," Paige reassured him, holding back a smile. She wished she could tell Chester what Jackson would look like one hundred years in the future, but knew it would sound unbelievable.

Quietly, they remained on the butte, observing the activity of the townspeople below. Some rode horses towards the outskirts of town. Others walked with arms full of supplies. After some time, Chester picked up the reins and signaled to the horse that it was time to go. Taking the same bumpy road back down, they returned to the livery barn, where Chester jumped down from his driver's seat and helped Paige out of the wagon.

She thanked him and then suddenly realized she must owe him a fee for his services.

"Oh, my," Paige exclaimed. "I'm sure I need to pay you something for the ride." She felt a sudden panic. She'd been unable to find any pockets when she'd picked up the Jackson's Hole Courier. It was unlikely she had any money.

Chester held his hand up and shook his head.

"No, ma'am," he replied. "You did me a favor, letting me take you to my favorite sittin' place. I'm the one who owes you a thank you. I know you're new to this here town. I hope you'll think to stop by again."

"I'll be sure to do that," Paige replied, not sure if this was a promise she'd be able to keep. Thanking him again, she crossed the barn, heading for the front door.

Just before she reached the exit, however, her attention was caught by some movement to her left. Looking over, she saw Jeremiah, from the saloon, working in one of the horse stalls. Surprised to see him again, she wandered over, causing him to look up as she approached.

"I just wanted to thank you again for your kindness in the saloon," Paige offered. "I'm not from around here and I'm afraid I don't know the local customs. I'm glad you were there."

"It was my pleasure," Jeremiah responded, tossing a slight grin in Paige's direction, while continuing to sweep up hay with a long-handled rake.

"I take it you work here," Paige said, wincing at the obvious as soon as the words crossed her lips.

"I help with the chores here a few times a week, cleaning stalls and feeding the horses." Jeremiah replied, setting the rake aside and lowering his voice. "Chester's getting on in years and can use an extra hand. Don't tell him I said so, though. He's got a hearty portion of pride."

He straightened up and attempted to brush his clothing down, though without much success. Loose strands of hay clung to his pant legs and smudges of dirt decorated his wrinkled shirtsleeves. Paige realized with a start how familiar his features were. He'd been wearing a hat inside the saloon and, sitting at the end of the bar, she hadn't noticed the resemblance at that time. But now, though his hair style and clothing were different, there was no question he looked very much like Jake.

Realizing she was staring, she stopped and offered an apology.

"I'm sorry to stare, it's just..." Paige paused. "It's just that you look very much like someone I know."

Jeremiah smiled, gathering his rake and other work supplies and heading across the barn to set them against the side wall.

"Thank you, ma'am," he said, after a pause. "I'm not sure if that's good or bad, but I'll take it as a compliment. At least I sure hope it is. It was a pleasure seein' you again, but I must be gittin' along now." He took his hat off a hook on the wall, tipped it towards Paige and turned away, crossing to the front of the barn.

Just before Jeremiah disappeared through the door, Paige saw something fall from his rear pocket. She walked quickly over to the spot to retrieve the item, intending to catch up with him to give it back. But when she came within several feet of the object, she stopped suddenly and stared. There, caught in a glimmer of light shining down from the barn's rafters, was the same skeleton key she had seen through the antler arch before. For a second she caught her breath and froze. Was it the arch that had brought her here, or the key itself? A fleeting quiver of fear ran through her as she realized there had been no antler arches around the dusty center block of town. There had to be a way to make sense out of what clearly seemed beyond reason. She just needed to find out what it was. Without even having to think twice, she stepped forward, reached down and grasped the key.

CHAPTER TEN

Jake didn't trust Frank. He didn't trust him at all, not at this point. For all he knew, Frank might have just given him another useless piece of paper. After downing the rest of his beer, he grabbed his hat and stood up. He ducked around a wayward cue stick, nodded a quick goodbye to Billy and stepped out onto the wooden slat sidewalk. Without wasting any time, he made his way back to his truck and headed towards the outskirts of town, slowing down just once to let late-season tourists saunter across the road.

Driving north through park territory, he hit the brakes sharply at one point to allow an elk to cross the highway and again, another mile later, to wait for a trio of deer to move off the road. He'd learned long ago to drive with extra caution, especially during twilight and evening hours. It was common for wildlife to cross the roads unexpectedly, often causing damage to vehicles, humans and wildlife alike. As eager as he was to look over the paper Frank had just given him, it wasn't worth the consequences of driving too quickly.

Turning east, he thought over the various interactions he'd had with Frank, from the first time he had been contacted by the old man right up to that evening's meeting at The Million Dollar Cowboy Bar. Was there any reason Frank might be feeding him false information? Is that what he'd been doing from the start? Maybe the map was a fake, the paper processed to appear old. Or maybe it was truly an original map, but had been altered somehow to throw him off track.

No, it didn't make sense. What would the motivation be? If the treasure didn't exist, Frank would've had no reason to bring him to Jackson. Was the buried gold real, but Frank was diverting him from the actual location with a map that wasn't authentic? That didn't make sense, either. Frank had clearly grown too old to search the mountains himself. And if he'd had someone else to do it, he wouldn't have come all the way up to Cody to plead for help.

Jake took a sharp left into the ranch driveway, screeching to a stop just long enough to let himself through the front gate. With a heavy foot on the gas pedal, gravel scattered sideways and clouds of dust billowed up behind him as he headed for the ranch house. Parking the truck abruptly, he jumped out, kicked the door shut and walked quickly inside, slamming the front door of the ranch house in the same manner. Whatever Frank was up to, he wasn't about to let him get away with it.

Grabbing the familiar book off the shelf, he pulled the first map out and unfolded it. He then took the new portion of the map out of his pocket and sat down in his chair, bringing the two together and studying them.

What had looked like a map on its own before had obviously just been part of a whole, as he had suspected. Together, the two pieces seemed to tell more of a story, though there was still much to figure out.

In the center of the map, where the two sides came together, it was now clear that the zigzag line continued into several sharp peaks of differing heights. These were almost identical to the shape of the Tetons. A winding line followed just to the right of the jagged lines, possibly a trail or stream or the boundary of a section of land. Several groupings of arrows were clustered in different areas. There appeared to be a plus sign in the center of the page, just to the right of the area where the two halves of the map connected. Perhaps it indicated that the map's sides should connect at that point. Or maybe it meant clues on both sides needed to be connected in order to determine the location.

There were no other markings to the left of the large zigzag and there was nothing to give any hints as to what the smudge on the right might mean. Jake still felt there must be something that tied the circular spot in with the rest of the marks. He had hoped to figure it out by piecing the map together, but so far it didn't make any more sense than before.

Additional lines and figures stretched across the bottom of the connected papers, but not in any way that clarified other parts of the map. Arrows, oval shapes, more zigzags and a set of short, parallel lines all seemed arbitrary. The haphazard smattering of shapes didn't appear to correspond with the other markings.

Jake set the two halves of the map aside. He considered taping them together, but thought better of it. The paper was yellowed and fragile and there were additional tears on both the left and right sides. No, it was best to keep them in two pieces and just bring them together whenever he needed to analyze them further.

Jake sat back and mulled over the chronology of his search. He'd been in the area for almost six months now. It had taken that long to settle in, blend in with the other townsfolk and to buy the ranch, so that he could be situated in the area where his great-grandfather had lived. He would be able to come and go with more privacy. The rest of his time had been devoted to searching for clues and scouting around to rule out some of the mountain areas as possible hiding places. He'd also spent endless hours researching the history of gold prospecting in Jackson Hole, knowing any knowledge could lead him a step closer to his goal.

What he hadn't had a chance to do was to get out and physically explore the area as much as he wanted to. He knew that knowledge of the trails, especially those that led into the Tetons, was crucial to his being able to discover the location of the gold. And now he had the map to provide clues. With this in mind, he returned both sections of the map to the hiding place in the bookcase and turned in for an early night's sleep, in order to be prepared for a day of trail exploration.

* * * *

It was clear and sunny when Jake stepped out into the crisp air the next morning. Travel mug of coffee in hand, he cranked up the truck and left the ranch, heading west toward the main highway. There were very few clouds in the sky, setting the valley dramatically against a stunning backdrop of blue. Three bison grazed along the north side of the road as Jake headed west to the main highway. A massive bull elk stood regally off to the left near Gros Ventre Junction, about fifty yards from the road. A six pointer, Jake surmised, noting the impressive rack of antlers.

Jake turned right on the highway and drove north to Moose, a tiny town consisting of a post office, a few stores off a side road and an impressive visitor center for Grand Teton National Park. He'd been to the visitor center many times since arriving in Jackson Hole, asking rangers questions about specific trails and analyzing the massive topographical map displayed in the lobby. This time he passed the visitor center without stopping and pulled up to the park's entrance gate, showing his annual pass to the ranger on duty. He smiled as he replaced the pass in his wallet. He'd been wise to cough up the fee for the annual pass when he first left Cody. It would be money well spent for the return he expected.

Continuing northbound through the park, he took in the flat, open fields on his right and the majestic Grand Tetons on his left. To the many people who visited the park each year, these mountains represented the strong, powerful forces of nature. To Jake, they represented much more.

He turned left at the south junction to Jenny Lake, a glacier-formed body of water estimated to date back 9,000 years. The road curved alongside low brush until it dropped off into the south parking area for the lake. Already into the off-season, it wasn't hard to find a parking space. He chose one near the front of the lot and pulled in, setting the parking brake and jumping out of the truck. He checked his small knapsack, which held a water bottle, trail mix, a pad of paper and a pen. He'd known better than to have brought the original map sections along, but had made a rough, handmade copy which contained all the major markings on the original papers.

He'd taken this trail several times before, when he'd first arrived in Jackson. His initial hikes were just out of curiosity and to get familiar with the area. Over time, though, he had come to suspect this section of the Tetons to be the probable location of the gold. The map now seemed to confirm this theory, based on the placement of the jagged lines in the center of the torn pieces. He was now determined to explore the trail and its immediate surroundings more thoroughly, looking for any landmarks that might resemble other markings on the map.

The boat dock on the edge of the lake was chained up and closed for the season, no longer offering a shortcut by ferry across the lake, as it did during summer months. Just as well, Jake thought. It would be better to explore the trail from the beginning, including the two mile section around the south side of the lake.

He crossed over Cottonwood Creek and started out on the trail. Engelmann Spruce and Alpine Fir filled much of the area, but there were also open sections of land off to his left where boulders and brush formed patches of natural landscaping. Frequent rocks protruded from the trail, pushing against Jake's feet as he moved forward. An occasional marmot peered out from under a cluster of rocks off to the side. A skittish deer ducked and ran for shelter when the approach of footsteps took it by surprise. To his right, the view across the still blue water of the lake was breathtaking. It was no wonder this was one of the most popular areas of the park for visitors and locals alike.

Not seeing anything in particular that resembled the markings on the map, Jake continued around the lake until the trail veered away from the water and started to climb. A series of switchbacks carried him higher in elevation. He stopped periodically to jot down notes about the surroundings – where the trail took a turn, where a large boulder was conspicuously situated and where certain trees stood out among others or were clustered together in groups. He recorded changes in the trail itself: a log set into the ground to form a step, a puddle of water that had formed from recent rain, a fallen tree and sections of the ground containing animal tracks. All current developments, he knew, none that would correspond with any marks on the map. But anything could be a potential clue, a sign that he was on the right track.

The trail continued at an incline, leveling off at times and then climbing again. As he neared Hidden Falls, he heard the faint sound of water crashing against rocks, but couldn't see the tumbling cascades until he rounded the last corner. It was clear that Hidden Falls was aptly named.

Jake continued to follow the trail as it began to climb more steeply, a narrow section of rock to his left. The right edge dropped off sharply and he took his steps carefully. He knew a tumble off the side could be deadly. Slowly moving along the path, he eventually reached the top of the incline, emerging onto a flat area with a dramatic view out over the lake and valley. This was Inspiration Point, a favorite hiking destination. He sat down to catch his breath and to take in the view.

Looking around, he ruled this out as a hiding place. It was far too visible. Even before the crowds started coming to Jackson Hole, before Yellowstone National Park drew visitors in by the millions, there would have been travel to this spot, both by Native American tribes and early settlers. It wasn't a likely place to leave anything that someone didn't want found.

He thought back to the way his grandfather had explained the legend. How he was certain that the gold had been both discovered and hidden, that it wasn't the ramblings of an even older man, Jake's great-grandfather. Grandpa Norris had been a little eccentric, which was one of the reasons others hadn't taken him seriously. But Jake had believed him from the first time he told the story of the gold that had been discovered by Great-Grandpa Norris and his prospecting partner. His grandfather had explained how his father's friend had hidden the gold himself, feeling it would be safer than the two of them hiking into the mountains together, which would have attracted more attention. After protesting, Great-Grandpa Norris conceded that it might be less obvious to have it hidden by one person. Whether out of extreme caution, or as an attempt to keep the gold for himself, the partner had stalled in telling Jake's great-grandfather where it had been hidden. As the story went, before he passed on this crucial information, the flood of 1927 had wiped out the town of Kelly, taking the only one who knew the hiding place out with it.

For many years, Jake had nothing much else to go on, only his grandfather's story and a vague description of what he believed to be the location – in the mountains, at some significant height above the valley floor. Jake had known the first time he looked at the immense expanse of the Grand Tetons that finding the gold wasn't going to be an easy task.

When Frank had contacted him the year before, he had been dubious, to say the least. To have a man drop out of nowhere, saying that he had been a friend of Jake's grandfather and had grown up with the same legend, just seemed too farfetched. That Frank's father had been the prospecting friend of Jake's great grandfather only made the whole story even harder to believe. But as Frank talked about the story as he had heard it growing up it began to closely resemble the one he had grown up with, as well. The more Jake thought about what a small world a sparsely populated area could be and the fact that some descendants of original pioneers still lived in the area, it became clear that it was indeed possible that two men from the same area could have fathers or grandfathers who were friends. Jake started to think Frank might be telling the truth.

Frank had said that he had tried for many years to locate the gold himself, following clues that had been passed on to him, just as similar clues had been passed on to Jake. But after decades of searching and finding nothing, the explorations became more difficult for him to carry out by himself. After one of several bad falls left him with a broken hip, Frank acquiesced to the fact that he was no longer the youthful explorer he had once been. The likelihood of his finding the gold now was growing slim and the physical ability to continue the search had become impossible. Still, Frank was determined to push on with efforts to find the gold. It might be too late for him to set up a full life of luxury now, but he certainly wouldn't mind living out his remaining years in style.

This is where Jake had come in. He was young enough to be able to continue the search. With luck, he'd be able to find it while Frank was still alive. With this in mind, he had tracked Jake down in Cody and struck a deal with him. Frank would pass on the information he had, including a map that had been discovered in a water tight box beneath the flooded, demolished house of his grandfather. Jake would provide the younger physical ability to do the searching himself. When the treasure was found, they would split the proceeds. It seemed a fair deal to them both, so Jake picked up and moved down to Jackson Hole.

Oddly, Frank had been less than forthcoming with information once Jake had arrived. He had suddenly been unable to find the map that he'd promised Jake. What's more, he seemed confused with details, which often contradicted each other in their daily conversations. Jake began pushing Frank for more information, threatening to give up the search altogether if Frank couldn't provide something more to go on.

It was Frank who had proposed meeting him in the town square, saying he would pass on the map, which had suddenly turned up during a thorough cleaning of his attic. It seemed he had conveniently remembered one or two other pieces of information, as well. Jake suspected this was still only a partial concession on Frank's part, which had caused the heated, and not too discreet, argument in the very public location. It was possible the old man's memory was just slipping, but it seemed more likely that he had held back the information.

It had taken some time, but his threat to give up the search, coupled with Frank's inability to continue searching himself, seemed to have finally worked. Jake now had the map in his possession. It was only a matter of figuring out the written clues and following them to the gold. This would be not only the culmination of a lifelong challenge for Jake, but the accomplishment of a dream that had lived for several generations. He had promised his grandfather that he would follow through and was not about to give up now. With this in mind, he stood up and began to climb higher.

Continuing on from Inspiration Point, the trail climbed slowly, running parallel to Cascade Creek. Jake paused now and then to take notes of formations of rocks or clusters of trees, as long as they appeared to have been part of the landscape for at least a century or more. He hiked deeper into the canyon, crossing Cascade Creek just before arriving at the Forks of Cascade Canyon, at which point he was faced with a choice. Turning left, he could follow the trail a little more than five miles to Hurricane Pass. To the right, just under three miles, was Lake Solitude. He weighed his options and chose the northern route, taking him to Lake Solitude. He could return another day to explore the other direction.

The climb was steeper than the section had been between Inspiration Point and the Forks of Cascade Canyon. The last mile consisted of steep switchbacks and Jake was winded by the time he reached the lake. Flanked by rocky cliffs, it was breathtakingly beautiful and worth the hike. But the likelihood the gold could be hidden behind this particular lake seemed unlikely, now that he stood facing it. Sheer rock surfaces around the lake's edge made it difficult to pass. Crossing the water would have required a boat, not easily brought to this height above the valley floor. On the front trail side of the lake, there weren't any rock formations or other clear possibilities for hiding places.

Jake ruled the location out and returned to the Forks. There wasn't enough time in the day to make it to Hurricane Pass and still get back down the mountain in daylight. He hadn't learned as much as he'd hoped, but he'd gained a few additional options to consider. In addition, he had been able to rule some areas out. With this as slight encouragement, he retraced his route down the trail to Jenny Lake, returned to his truck and headed back toward the ranch.

CHAPTER ELEVEN

A brisk wind rustled through the trees and then died down as Paige shook her head and glanced around. Looking first in each of her open hands and then down at the ground, there was no sign of the skeleton key. Checking her pockets, she also came up empty. Dazed, she found her way to a bench and sat down to catch her breath and collect her thoughts.

Evening was quickly falling on Jackson and the temperature had grown chilly. The town square was brimming with activity. Tiny lights twinkled along the rooftops of small boutiques and art galleries. Bright lights flooded restaurant entrances, welcoming evening diners. Cars passed by on the streets and a row of Harleys lined a portion of the curb. Small clusters of people filled corners, waiting for green lights to announce open crosswalks. It was a busy scene, an active scene and a very different scene from that of 1909.

Paige glanced around, stopping to rest her eyes on the neon cowboy sign above the Million Dollar Cowboy Bar. Though not one for the bar scene in general, a good, stiff drink sounded pretty good at the moment. She stood, straightened herself up, patted back her hair and marched across the square. Grateful to be back in her jeans and sweater and not stuffed into a showy, breath-stealing dress, she crossed Cache St. and entered the bar.

It was crowded inside and the famous saddles were all occupied. A flurry of activity surrounded the pool tables and Paige ducked around more than one cue stick while trying to cross the floor. In the far corner, a live band twanged out a rendition of a Garth Brooks tune. Several couples danced in front of the stage and cocktail waitresses maneuvered trays around the room, taking orders and delivering drinks. Glasses clinked toasts against each other and empty beer bottles were whisked from tables, switched out quickly for icy replacements. Bursts of laughter broke out as a good joke made its way around the bar.

Seeing a saddle open up at the counter, Paige seized the opportunity and grabbed the seat. As crowded as it was in the busy establishment, she had to wave several times at the bartender before she could catch his attention and order a drink. Finally the welcome sight of a dry martini landed in front of her, a twist of lemon adding a festive edge to the chilled glass.

As she took the first few sips of blended vodka and vermouth, she became aware of a man in the next seat. He faced away from her and seemed oblivious not only of Paige, but of most everyone around him, other than a stocky woman wearing a dark brown leather jacket and a hat that hid her face. Both appeared to have had quite a bit to drink, enough to carelessly raise their voices and allow portions of their conversation to float back to Paige.

"This had better not backfire," the woman hissed, a tone of impatience in her voice.

The man lifted his beer to his mouth, tilting his head back while he took several gulps. He waved his hand sloppily in front of him, as if swatting at a fly.

"Quit your nagging," he responded, as annoyed as he could sound while under the influence of many a beer already consumed. "I told you he'll fall for it. He already fell for the first one. You're worrying for nothing. Besides, you're the one who asked for my help, so just shut up and leave me alone."

"You're taking a big risk, giving him so much information," she continued with an angry huff. "We could end up with nothing."

The man slapped his hand down on the bar, briefly attracting the attention of nearby customers. He waited for them to return to their own conversations before lowering his voice to counter the woman's latest statement.

"You're wrong. This Jake kid isn't that smart," the man said, slurring his words. "He'll lead us to it, but that's it. It's not like he's an expert on prospecting or anything. He doesn't know enough to screw up your stupid plan. Now stop your worrying and leave the rest up to me."

The woman leaned in closer to the man, lowering her voice to a cross between a whisper and a threat.

"OK," she sneered. "We'll do it your way. But you'd better be right about this."

The man set his glass down on the bar a little too hard, enough to cause the bartender to glance over. Shrugging his shoulders and shaking his head, he stood up and turned around, threw some money on the counter and walked out the door.

The woman waited until he had left the bar, turning her head once to check the door to make sure he was gone. She then stood and took her own exit, Paige's surprised gaze following her across the floor. It didn't make sense, but Paige knew what she had seen. The woman had been Maddie, from the Blue Sky Café. And the man had been Old Man Thompson.

CHAPTER TWELVE

Jake reached the junction of Hwy 89 and started to turn south to head back to the ranch. Impulsively, though, he twisted the steering wheel to the left and drove north. Looking west, the outline of the mountains changed slightly as he continued to drive. But the impressive stance of the Tetons never diminished. These mountains were breathtaking from any direction.

Jake thought about the markings on the map, about the smoother flow of the winding line to the right of the sharper, jagged zigzag. The placement of the line had to indicate something east of the mountain range, though how far east was difficult to tell. There was nothing on the map that indicated a roadway, though certainly there had already been one through the central valley at that time. Yellowstone had already become a popular destination in the 1800's and trade to the north would have had to move in that direction, as well.

Pulling over at Snake River Overlook, he parked his truck and walked out to the observation area. The view was magnificent with the mountains towering directly before him. Pine trees lined the edge of the valley, which stretched flat until it reached the mountains. There was no gradual change here, no foothills separating the valley floor from the tall peaks. The shifting of the earth's layers over the years had forced sharp, abrupt changes in the displaced sections of ground. Where the flat valley ended, the mountains soared instantly into the sky.

Looking out from the overlook, Jake saw what he had expected to find. The Snake River's path took one of its many dramatic twists at this location, flowing in from the north and almost doubling back on itself before straightening out again. This ribbon shape resembled the winding line on the map. And, looking across the valley, the river seemed to point toward the general area of Jenny Lake before continuing south. Picture perfect, Jake mused. There was little wonder why Ansel Adams chose this particular spot for one of his photos for The Mural Project in 1941-42.

Mulling over the similarities between the winding line on the map and the curves of the Snake River, Jake returned to his truck and drove south, pausing just once to allow an elk to cross the highway. Upon reaching the ranch, he parked the truck and entered the ranch house, flinging his hat onto the hook inside the door. Without hesitation, he poured himself a glass of brandy and settled into the wing-backed chair. Watching the last rays of the sun stretch across the land, he ran his impressions from the day around in his head. As his eyelids grew heavy, he set the drink down on a side table. Giving in to the fatigue from the day's explorations and the comfort of his favorite chair, he drifted off to sleep.

CHAPTER THIRTEEN

Paige waited until Maddie and Old Man Thompson were gone before leaving the bar herself. It wouldn't help for them to realize she had been there, especially close enough to overhear. Luckily the liquor appeared to have prevented this. For that, Paige was thankful. Not only might she have been in danger if she had been recognized, but it would certainly make it harder to get her morning lattes. And those lattes had now positioned themselves as investigative opportunities.

In sorting through the bits and pieces of conversation she had overheard, she was starting to think Jake could be in serious trouble. Maddie and Old Man Thompson had mentioned prospectors. Was this about gold? Maybe they simply wanted him to lead them to something and would leave him alone once he found it, but that didn't seem likely. For one thing, they hardly sounded trustworthy. In addition, they might think Jake could track them once he discovered they had tricked him. She doubted they were planning to leave loose ends. This made her nervous. On the other hand, a wave of excitement ran through her. If her hunches were correct, the pieces were starting to come together.

Exhausted from the events of the day, she returned to her car, parked across the street from the Blue Sky Café. Weary, she drove north to Gros Ventre Junction and then east to her cabin. Too tired to even turn on the light, she shed her clothes, leaving them heaped on the floor and fell into her bed. Within minutes she was sound asleep.

She slept deeply for half the night, but woke with a start at three o'clock in the morning, bolting upright and breathing heavily, trying to catch her breath. A panic attack, she thought, feeling her heart pounding. Just breath in and out, it will pass. She stood up and walked around the cabin in the dark, her mind racing as she tried to pull her thoughts together. Portions of dreams floated back to her, glimpses of the events of the previous day that blurred together in confused scenes. Present day people were walking down the street in the past. The dance hall existed in the present. Maddie and Old Man Thompson were dancing at Tuttle's Saloon. Chester was playing pool at The Million Dollar Cowboy Bar.

It was all so confusing, not at all what she had expected when she came to Jackson Hole to write a simple article. Maybe she was in danger, as well. Perhaps she would be better off leaving for home right away, before things became even more complicated. Instead of getting in any deeper, she could be sitting in her Manhattan apartment, finishing a basic draft on Jackson Hole's history. But she already knew that wasn't going to happen. She was too caught up already.

She sat in the dark for the rest of the night, until the glow of sunlight began to rise over the mountains to the east. She made a pot of coffee, quickly downed a cupful and returned to the back room, where she retrieved the clothes she had cast off the night before. Hanging her jacket on one of the wall hooks that served as closet space, she tossed the rest into a makeshift hamper on the floor. Picking up her boots next to move them out by the front door, she felt a shiver run through her as her hand touched a crisp edge of paper.

Reaching inside, she slowly pulled out a copy of the Jackson's Hole Courier dated Oct. 23, 1909. Stunned, she quickly tucked it away in a pocket inside her jacket, dressed as rapidly as possible and headed into town.

She hesitated before going to the Blue Sky Café for her usual morning latte, but it seemed silly to avoid the place. She was certain Maddie and Old Man Thompson had not seen her in the bar the night before. Besides, now that she knew they were involved, her visits to the café could provide opportunities for obtaining additional information.

Maddie was behind the counter, as usual, when Paige entered the café. She seemed exceptionally friendly as she handed over the vanilla latte, accompanied by a cinnamon scone that Paige had picked out from inside the glass display. But she also appeared tired, her face a little drawn, slight bags under her eyes. True to his daily routine, Old Man Thompson sat in his usual place, not looking up. Paige took her favorite seat near the front corner and browsed through the local paper. With the old copy of the 1909 paper safely tucked inside her jacket, the current morning paper took on a whole new perspective.

The café was quiet, only serving up beverages and assorted muffins or bagels to a handful of customers who stopped by. Between orders, Maddie worked intently on preparations for baking. Old Man Thompson, as always, stayed at the counter and stared into his coffee. There was no interaction between them, other than one occasion when Maddie reached over the counter and refilled his coffee cup.

Paige drank half of her latte while sitting in the café and then took the rest to go, sipping it while she drove to the library. There she took her turn at the computer, logged in and pulled up her email. She hesitated before sending an update off to Susan this time. It wouldn't do any good to

report events that would seem unbelievable. She needed the
email to sound at least somewhat rational.

To: Susan Shaw
From: Paige Mackenzie

Re: Jackson Hole Article

Hi Susan,

*I've had some excitement the last couple days. It may sound
incredible, but I have reason to believe there is a stash of gold
hidden in this valley. What's more, I think a couple of the locals
are very close to finding it. Obviously this would make an
amazing story. I'd like to stay and see this through, if there aren't
any other assignments pending. Otherwise, I've obtained quite
an insight into the history of the area. I could return and do a
historical piece, if you prefer. But, if possible, I'd like to continue
to follow my hunch about the gold.*

Please advise!

Paige

Paige leaned against the back of the wooden chair and
almost laughed out loud at her wording. "Quite an insight"
was certainly an understatement. But what else could she say?
Her recent method of historical information-gathering was a
bit more intensive than the usual techniques she used for
research. It was far wiser to leave this out of her report. She
had no intention of turning this trip into a visit to a mental
health facility.

There was no one in line for the computer, so Paige
lingered to run a few Google searches. She found a photo of

the town taken in 1907 by William Trester, reportedly the first. It showed a town square virtually identical to the one she had seen after stepping through the antler arch. A few small buildings were missing, undoubtedly built over the next two years as the town grew. But otherwise it appeared the same.

She searched a few more areas on the Internet, reading up on the history of gold prospectors in the valley, including specific locations they had explored. All accounts said that little was ever discovered. Paige looked for anything that might confirm the things she had seen and heard the last couple days, but there was nothing.

She closed out the search windows on the computer and checked her email box again. As she suspected, knowing Susan was an early riser and already at her desk, there was an email response already waiting.

To: Paige Mackenzie
From: Susan Shaw

Re: Jackson Hole Article

Paige,

Wow, great news. This would make an amazing exclusive, if your hunch turns out to be right. With you right there in Jackson Hole, we could get the news before it hits the wires. Don't even think about coming back before exhausting the search for more information. This is a story we need. It could be a big break for your career. Stay at it and keep me posted. Keep digging.

Susan

The response was exactly what Paige had expected. Even better, it gave her an excuse to stay longer in Jackson Hole. She logged off the computer and left the library. Half way to her car, she paused, returned to the library and asked the information desk if they had any topographical maps. She was directed to a file cabinet of sorts, but with long, narrow horizontal drawers. She opened the top one and rummaged through some flat, laminated maps, all about two feet by three. Finding one of the lower valley and surrounding mountains, she pulled it out and carried it to a nearby table, where she placed it under the light.

The open portion of the valley clearly appeared flat, a wide expanse with markings for rivers, lakes and national forest and park boundaries. As the flat land approached the mountains on either side, curved lines indicated ridges and altitude changes. Lakes and trails were specifically marked. Smaller landmarks were not. It was going to take information from several sources to pull everything together.

It was against library policy to check out certain reference materials, including the maps. Paige made a few notes and placed the map back in its drawer, looking around her as she pushed it shut. It was odd how ill at ease she seemed to feel all of a sudden, though she hadn't done anything wrong.

She attempted to sort through her thoughts while driving away from the library. It was still possible that she was chasing nothing at all. Stopping at the town square, she walked through the area, but there was nothing to give her any extra clues. The antler arches stood solid and gray against a cloudy sky. There was no hint of a glow on the corner arch near the café. There was no skeleton key anywhere on the ground and no mysterious meetings taking place near any of the benches.

Seemingly normal activity continued in front of the surrounding shops, cafes and galleries. Shoppers emerged from stores carrying bags of purchases. Potential dinner customers browsed posted menus outside restaurants, surveying dining options. Gallery window displays caught the attention of art aficionados as they passed by. Nothing seemed off or out of place, other than the thoughts and experiences Paige held inside her. A dull headache began to form as she tried to process everything. No matter how she looked at all the pieces, they simply fell into a heap of confusion when she tried to make sense of them.

A feeling of uneasiness started building inide as she questioned how to start pulling the scattered bits of information together. It was not going to be easy. She tossed the jumbled thoughts around as she left the square and headed for the cabin, stopping only on the outskirts of town for some Advil to tackle the ache that continued to creep across her forehead. Impulsively, she added a package of hot cocoa to her purchase, hoping something warm and sweet would help ease the oncoming headache and sooth her nerves.

Back in the car, she continued north. Elk were just beginning to come down from higher altitudes to graze for the winter in the safety of the National Elk Refuge. Beyond the refuge, tall mountains stood against the eastern horizon, with snow capping the highest sections. Though they were less dramatic than the Grand Tetons to the west, they were still impressive.

As she turned right at Gros Ventre Junction and headed for the cabin, she began to feel increasingly uneasy. What if Jake really was in danger? What if she had the knowledge to warn him and she held back? What would happen to him? Would she be responsible? She argued with herself that this was really none of her business. She had come to Jackson

Hole simply to do an article and she'd be better off not getting involved personally. Yet she knew it was too late for that. She was already involved.

She struggled back and forth with these thoughts as she continued east. Fields of bison surrounded the curved slopes of Blacktail Butte. Pine-flanked mountains rose up beyond the town of Kelly. She took these images in absent-mindedly, her energy drawn to the conflicting feelings running through her head. She aimed for the cabin, approaching the driveway and signaling to turn in. But at the last minute, just as she was starting the turn, she surprised herself by jerking the wheel back onto the road and driving toward Jake's ranch.

CHAPTER FOURTEEN

Jake moved from the chair to the bed sometime in the middle of the night and slept soundly until long after the sun had risen. Yet, in spite of sleeping well, he woke up with the blurry feeling of sleep deprivation, making him suspect that he hadn't slept as soundly as he thought he had. Thinking a good breakfast would help do the trick, he got the coffee maker started and tossed two slices of honey wheat bread in the toaster. After a brief inspection of his refrigerator's contents, he pulled out eggs, cheese and green onions, grated the cheese, sliced the onions and scrambled it all together in a large, iron pan. Retrieving his toast from the toaster, he slapped everything on a plate and sat in front of the kitchen's westward facing window.

He spread some orange marmalade on his toast, looking beyond his property, across the valley and over to the Grand Tetons. This was the distance that separated him from the gold. He got up to pour a second cup of coffee and then sat down again, slowly stretching his legs and arms and then finishing his breakfast with a surprisingly avid hunger. He set the dishes in the sink and retreated to the living room, where, as seemed to always be the case now, he pulled the map out and sat down to analyze it again. There was always a chance he might find something he had missed before.

This time he inspected the smaller markings, those that were so minor that they hadn't seemed to warrant much attention. He knew already from the zigzag of the line on the left that the map was set in a typical north to south, east to west format. This placed the town of Jackson at the lower edge of the map.

There were several additional marks along the bottom that appeared to indicate the town, scratchy marks that looked like scrub brush, a few squares that appeared to be buildings, and some short parallel lines that looked like either a ladder or maybe a path. Or some sort of crossing, perhaps a wooden sidewalk or even the slats of a wall. There were a number of possibilities. An oval shape seemed to indicate a body of water, though that didn't make sense to Jake. There wasn't a lake that close to the town area. He considered the possibility that there used to be one and that it had dried up over the years since the map was made. But he was more inclined to believe it represented something else, though he couldn't venture a guess as to what it was.

He was sure the gold wasn't buried near the town itself, which made the lower markings on the map unimportant. They simply set the location of the town and indicated the northward direction from there. He was still on the right track. The curving line down the center of the page represented the Snake River, just as it had appeared from Snake River Overlook. It veered in the direction of Jenny Lake. Yes, he was certain he had it right. Now he just had to follow through until he found the exact location.

Jake was getting ready to put the map away when he was startled by a knock on the door. He'd never had visitors, not since he'd moved from Cody. He'd made it a point to keep his distance from the local people, appearing friendly while in town, but reclusive once outside. It was his protection, his way to avoid having anyone guess his motivation for coming to Jackson Hole. Other than Frank Thompson, no one knew why he was here. And Frank would never tell anyone. He had too much to lose.

Quickly Jake stashed the map back in the shelf, making sure it was completely hidden before crossing to the front door. He suspected a car had broken down or perhaps someone had become disoriented driving around the valley and needed directions. But he did not expect to open the door and find the girl from the library standing on the porch. With so much on his mind, he hadn't had time to think of their brief, awkward encounter over flying books.

What he did remember, though, was her shiny, auburn hair, as well as her trim figure and rich-toned, hazel eyes. These same eyes now held a look that was a cross between embarrassment and anxiety, nervous and flustered at the same time. But they still held the depth that he recalled from their last meeting.

Paige attempted to speak, then closed her mouth and shook her head. She appeared to collect her thoughts again and ventured another effort.

"I'm Paige Mackenzie, I met you at the library," she attempted. "Well, it's probably more accurate to say I bumped into you." She shook her head sheepishly. To her relief, Jake laughed.

"Yes, I seem to recall that I was on my way to check out a few books and, just as I turned away from the shelf to head toward the counter, you flew around the corner at the speed of lightening and just about knocked the both of us over." He crossed his arms and smiled, watching her for a reaction.

Paige felt slightly annoyed at this exaggeration and contemplated turning around and leaving. But she had come to talk to him and had ventured too far already to not see it through. She gathered her composure and spoke up.

"I know this is going to sound odd, in fact it's going to sound far-fetched," she began, her voice trailing off. "Actually, the honest truth is it's probably going to sound like I've lost my mind, which may very well be the case." This just wouldn't do, Paige thought to herself. Now she was babbling. A sudden urge to disappear into thin air flashed though her mind. That is, until she remembered she had apparently done exactly that not very long ago.

Jake stood watching as Paige fumbled for words. She was pretty, more than pretty. She was beautiful, in fact, with classic features and a soft complexion, Jake found it difficult to pay attention to what she was saying, though it didn't appear at first that she was saying much of anything at all. Babbling had never been impressive to him, but somehow in Paige it seemed cute. He shifted his weight and waited for her to explain the point of her unexpected visit. It was almost enjoyable, watching her struggle to get words out.

There was nothing enjoyable, however, once she managed to speak up. His expression changed immediately as he listened to the words pour out. Jake straightened up quickly, grabbed Paige by the arm and pulled her inside, closing the door with enough force that it made Paige a little fearful.

"What did you just say?" Jake demanded, continuing to hold her by the arm, making Paige wince a little with discomfort, until Jake realized he was hurting her and let go.

Paige took a deep breath and repeated the words she had spoken outside on the porch.

"I said I think you're in danger. I overheard a man mention your name and it sounded…," she searched for the right words. "It sounded threatening. I know I don't know you, but I think you're in danger. I just came here because I wanted to warn you."

Jake stood back and looked at Paige with a puzzled expression, the only cover he could pull up for the actual worry that was starting to mount. How could she possibly know anything? After all, he had only seen her around town for a week or so. He waited quietly for her to continue and then listened carefully as she spoke.

"I was in The Cowboy Bar the other night," Paige started off, "You know, the one near the town square with the neon…" She paused as Jake nodded and waved for her to go on.

"Well, anyway, I had a rough…I mean an unusual…I mean…a very strange day and had decided a drink sounded good." Paige paused to take a breath. Jake fought off the passing thought that a drink was actually starting to sound good to him right now, his recent breakfast notwithstanding.

"And then what happened," Jake pressed, growing impatient.

"I took a seat on one of those saddles. You know how they have saddles in there, instead of…" She stopped again, watching Jake's expression grow weary. He didn't even need to motion for her to continue this time.

"Anyway," she hurried up, as much out of nervousness being near Jake as out of her need to get the story out, "I sat down next to a man who had his back toward me. He'd had quite a few drinks already and he didn't seem to know I was there. He was rambling on a little and occasionally slamming his fist down on the counter, that sort of thing. No one seemed to pay that much attention to him. I assumed he was a local and that people were used to him being there."

Jake moved back and took a seat, watching Paige intently as she continued.

Paige started pacing slowly in front of Jake's chair, thinking through the conversation and motioning with her arms as she attempted to reconstruct it for Jake.

"He was telling the woman not to worry, that he had it all under control. He said your name, Jake. He said "Jake fell for the first one and he'll fall for the second." He also said you would lead them to it – whatever it is, that part he didn't say – but that you wouldn't get it. That's what he told her."

Jake shook his head and held both of his hands out flat in front of him, confused. "That's what he told her? Told who?"

"The woman who was standing next to him," Paige explained. "You know her, Maddie, the one who runs the Blue Sky Café." She paused a minute. "He never said her name, but I recognized her. Oh, and she called him Frank."

Jake stood up and walked across the room, avoiding Paige's eyes. He continued into the kitchen, where Paige thought she heard the sound of a dull thud. When he returned, however, he looked calmer and casually took his seat again.

"Look," he said slowly, a forced smile across his face, "I really do appreciate you trying to warn me about whatever it was they were talking about. But I'm afraid you've got the wrong person. I haven't a clue what this is about."

"But the man said, 'Jake,'" Paige insisted. "I heard that clearly, even over the clanking of pool balls and beer bottles, even over the music in the background. He definitely said your name."

Jake stood and nodded to her with a reassuring expression. "I'm sure he did, but this town isn't as small as it used to be and Jake's a pretty common name these days. I'm sorry for whoever it is who's in trouble with them, but you've got the wrong guy."

Frustrated and more than slightly exasperated, Paige shook her head and walked toward the front door. Jake jumped up and turned the doorknob before she could reach it, holding the door open in a gentlemanly fashion.

"I'm sorry," she muttered, discouraged and embarrassed. It had been worth the try. Maybe he was right, after all. Maybe they were talking about a different Jake.

"I'm sorry, too," Jake said with a kind expression on his face. "I know you were trying to help." He studied her face a minute, waiting for her to depart. He refrained from adding what he was thinking, though - that he wasn't at all sorry to have seen her again.

CHAPTER FIFTEEN

Jake paced back and forth, trying not to panic. He had played it off well enough in front of Paige. There had been nothing to make her think that her comments had hit a nerve, other than the mug he had clumsily knocked off the kitchen table in a short burst of anger. But that surely sounded like an accident. She hadn't mentioned it when he returned to the main room. No, she wasn't a problem.

Frank, however, was definitely a problem. For one thing, Jake had counted on him to be discreet. The last thing they needed was to have other treasure seekers coming out of the woodworks. This belonged to their families and they were the ones who deserved to find it. On the other hand, if Frank had intentions of tricking Jake and keeping the gold for himself, he had another thing coming. This didn't worry Jake as much. He knew the old man was no match for him, not mentally or physically. He just had to be more careful. And he'd need to be less forthcoming with reports of progress than he had been up to now, since he suspected Frank was no longer to be trusted.

What troubled him the most was hearing that Maddie was somehow involved. Why would Frank have kept this a secret? All those mornings at the Blue Sky Café he had been served coffee by the seemingly innocent, well-meaning woman. Had she been behind the plan to recover the gold all along? Perhaps even before Frank asked him to come down to Jackson?

His mind raced through these new pieces of information, trying to formulate a plan. For whatever reason he had overlooked Frank's inner motives before, he now had his eyes wide open. If Frank truly had plans to double cross him, he wasn't about to let him get away with it.

He was going to need a way to hide information from Frank now, but without it seeming suspicious. If he could keep two searches going – one the actual track he was on and another, a false one, to report to Frank - that could work to throw him off. And considering Frank was unaware that Jake suspected he was up to something, Jake was at an advantage, something he owed to Paige.

Thinking of this brought Paige to mind. He'd noticed her even before the awkward run-in at the library. She'd been at the Blue Sky Café one morning, sitting in the far corner with her morning coffee, or one of those trendy coffee drinks that were so popular now. Writing in a journal of sorts, she hadn't appeared to see him from across the room. But a pretty, new girl in town was hard to miss.

He'd looked away before she could notice and had made a point of not looking back again, even when he walked out the door. Women were always trouble of one kind or another. Even when she bumped into him at the library he'd resisted the urge to talk to her more, though the temptation to ask her out for coffee or perhaps even dinner had crossed his mind at the time.

Now that she was somehow connected to this whole situation, he was worried. It might not be enough to just keep his distance. She was clearly the determined sort, not the type to give up on anything easily. He was going to have to keep an eye on her now, to make sure she didn't cause problems with his plans. In addition, he realized he was starting to feel concerned for her safety, as well as his own. It didn't sound like Frank and Maddie were aware she had overheard them talking, but if they found out she had, she could very well be in danger. He was going to have to figure a way to keep her out of the middle of all this. The only question was how.

He stepped out onto the front porch and looked up at the sky, watching the sun continue to rise. Everything had suddenly become complicated. Now he'd have to juggle different people's motives. He'd also need to devise a decoy story, which was going to take careful thinking and planning. What was also clear was that he'd have to deal with Paige one way or another. This he contemplated the longest, leaning against a post at the edge of the porch and thinking over his options. In the end, he realized there was only one way to really keep an eye on her. He was going to have to be around her more. Against his will, a slow smile came to his face.

CHAPTER SIXTEEN

Frustrated from the conversation with Jake, Paige drove back to the cabin and parked the car, slamming the door a little too hard and letting the front door of the cabin bang a bit too harshly, as well. She had done her best to offer Jake help, but if he wasn't going to take it, there was nothing she could do.

She built a fire and settled down in front of it, surrounding herself with notes and research. A hearty session of writing rarely failed to take her mind off a stressful situation. As the flames warmed the small cabin, she began to relax. After all, she hadn't come to Jackson to get involved with all this. Nor was she here to save townspeople from other townspeople. If Jake was going to be stubborn about things, that really didn't have to be her concern. A feeling of relief accompanied these thoughts. She could choose whether or not to be involved. The logical choice was to stay clear.

Pulling out her laptop, she worked in front of the fire, outlining a basic article. Hours flew by as Paige wove area history and culture together into chronological order. Relaxed from the process of writing undisturbed, she was more than a little startled to hear a knock on the door. Certain it was Dan, she set the laptop aside, rose to her feet and walked across the cabin to answer the door.

To her surprise, she found Jake standing on the porch. He appeared a little bashful, a look she begrudgingly had to admit was appealing. Unable to hide the fact that she was surprised to see him, she returned the slight smile and simply waited for him to speak.

"I was on my way into town and saw your car in the driveway here," he said, crossing his arms across his chest and rocking back on his heels. "So I thought I ought to stop and thank you, however wrong you were, for trying to help me or warn me or whatever it was you were trying to do earlier."

Feeling a chilly gust of wind blow in from the porch, Paige waved him inside, indicating her work area in front of the fire. He accepted the offer and stepped into the cabin, nodding with approval at its quaint, inviting atmosphere.

"I have a fireplace at the ranch, but I always seem to forget to use it," he sighed. "Just not in the habit, I guess." He leaned forward and rubbed his hands together, absorbing the warmth of the flames.

Paige smiled softly. "I love the fireplace here. It's one of the reasons I took the cabin. I'd been staying at the Sweet Mountain Inn, but this was more remote and more conducive to writing." She pointed to the floor, an unspoken suggestion to sit down, which they both did.

"I take it you're a writer, then," Jake asked, taking a seat on the floor.

"I do features about small towns for a newspaper back east. Local stories, that sort of thing," Paige replied, "And sometimes a bit of investigative reporting."

Jake laughed. "I see," he said. "Then that explains a few things."

"Such as?" Paige answered, hoping she was about to draw him into revealing some sort of information.

Again Jake laughed. "Such as why you would come up with crazy notions about mysterious local situations." He watched as she rolled her eyes, looking half annoyed and half resigned to him holding back. Though she still firmly believed that her hunches were correct, she was willing to play along. If he wasn't going to open up to her now, she couldn't push it. When the time was right, she'd be able to break through his façade.

Noticing the fire was almost out, Paige stood up to put more wood on the glowing embers. As she moved, her hair swung casually across her shoulders, something Jake didn't miss noticing.

"Wait, I have an idea," he said quickly, causing her to stop before setting the wood in the fireplace. "I was just on my way into town to get a bite to eat. Why don't you ride along with me? We could get something easy." He watched for her reaction.

Paige found herself taken by surprise at this suggestion. Everything she had seen from Jake so far had indicated that he was a loner. It seemed odd that he was suddenly expressing an interest in having a meal together. At the same time, however, she had to admit to feeling a little flutter of excitement. She set the wood back in the stack to the side of the fireplace and used a poker to move the embers around into safe positions. She told Jake his suggestion sounded like a great idea.

Already growing familiar with Wyoming, she grabbed her heavy rain jacket from a hook by the door. There wasn't any way to predict the weather from one hour to the next. Besides, it was already cool and, once the sun set, the temperature would drop rapidly. Taking a warm jacket was a good precaution.

The drive into town was relaxing, aside from an unspoken current that ran between them. With Jake at the wheel, Paige was able to see more of the landscape than she had been able to on her solo trips into town. The open land reached out across the valley with a serenity that ended in the splash of the mountain backdrop, a river of soft, brown grasses and wildflowers that turned dramatically into steep slabs of granite.

Talking seemed to come easily. Jake told stories of growing up in Cody, the land of Buffalo Bill. He had helped his father raise cattle and had attended local schools. He'd learned to ride horses at an early age and had even tried his hand at bronco riding. It was a life very different from hers and she found it fascinating.

Paige responded with descriptions of New York City, which Jake found almost impossible to imagine. Each story she told of crowded streets and skyscrapers, of taxis and the melting pot of different people, brought a look of amazement to his face. It was so different from anything he had known.

"Well, I guess you'd never feel alone in a place like that," he ventured, trying to imagine the hectic pace of life that she had described.

"Actually, I think many people there feel very lonely," she responded, to his surprise. "There's an impersonal feeling to city life. There are so many people that it seems we all get lost in the crowd. I think I've felt more alone there than anywhere I've ever visited." She stopped and thought about this, only realizing how true it was as she described it.

They found a parking space easily once they entered town. Jake locked the truck and the two walked along the wooden sidewalk, debating options for food. Finally deciding on a small Mexican restaurant, they were soon seated beside a wall covered with brightly painted hibiscus. A basket of chips quickly landed on the table, two cups of salsa alongside – one mild and one referred to by the server as "fire," which Jake pushed to the far side of the table as he quickly shook his head at Paige in warning.

Without looking at a menu, Jake suggested fajitas for both of them, an idea Paige agreed to readily. Layering sautéed chicken, fresh chopped lettuce, grilled onions, peppers and guacamole into soft, warm flour tortillas, they continued to exchange stories about their very different lives, keeping the conversation casual.

Over coffee and flan, however, Paige pushed a little more about the conversation she had overheard between Frank and Maddie the night before.

"Really," Jake responded, almost too abruptly. "I think this investigative reporting has gotten a hold on your imagination." Seeing Paige's injured look, he continued on quickly in a softer tone. "What I mean is that it has to be hard to separate what is real from what isn't. That must be one of the challenges of your type of work."

On this Paige had to agree. On more than one occasion she had fallen into conflicting information and had to sort out the truth from distorted facts. However, she felt certain that this wasn't one of those times. Jake was obviously not going to reveal anything to her readily, but at least he was making an effort to be friendly, which could work to her advantage. She'd have to be patient, but she had a hunch that she'd get him to cave in. In addition, though she hated to admit it, she felt drawn to him more and more.

Finishing up, Jake paid the bill and they started back towards the truck. But as Jake started to pull his keys out to open the door for her, he suddenly grabbed her arm and pulled her back into the doorway of a small shop. Surprised at the sudden movement, she looked at him for an explanation. Silently he held one finger up to his lips, while cupping his other hand over her mouth. Confused, but trusting that he knew what he was doing, Paige nodded, allowing him to lower his hands and pull her farther back into the shadows.

Huddling motionless inside the recessed doorway, Paige could now hear footsteps approaching. It sounded at first like those of one person, but as the sound came closer it became clear there were two people walking together. Hushed voices accompanied the sound of the feet on the sidewalk and both sounds were growing closer.

Paige cast a nervous glance at Jake's face, just inches away from hers. She could feel his breath against her cheek and his arm holding her close to his side. He returned the look with an unspoken message that they needed to stay silent. She followed his advice, which turned out to be a wise decision. Even before the people came into view, she recognized the voices as those of Frank and Maddie.

"Damn it, Maddie," Frank said angrily. "I wish you'd get off my case. I know what I'm doing."

"So you say, Lou" Maddie snapped back.

"Don't call me that," Frank threatened. "You're gonna slip one of these days and screw up your own plan. So far this is working just fine. No one knows about Frank's unfortunate accident." His voice stabbed sarcastically at each syllable.

"Of course not," Maddie whispered. "That was four states and five decades ago. Besides, Aunt Ruby was too clever for that, which is more than I can say for you. I'm paying you well, so you'd better make this work."

"Look, the map was passed down directly from Ruby herself, at least that what you claim," Frank hissed in a hushed tone. "There's no better source. Now hold your horses and let Jake finish up. Then we'll take care of him. And that little out of town trouble-maker, too…"

The voices faded away as the footsteps continued on down the street. When they could no longer be heard, Jake motioned for Paige to stay in the shadows while he walked quickly to the truck and opened the door, signaling for Paige to climb in. As she did, he ran to the other side and jumped into the driver's seat. Silently, they both stared straight ahead, neither one saying a word. Finally, Jake spoke up.

"I guess maybe I'd better tell you what's going on," he said quietly.

Paige nodded her head in the dark, still shaking from the close call.

"Yeah," she replied slowly. "I think that would be a good idea."

CHAPTER SEVENTEEN

The moon was three quarters full, and shining brightly through the truck window, when Paige and Jake reached the ranch. They'd ruled out stopping at The Million Dollar Cowboy Bar. Conversation there was too risky, as Paige had found out so recently. Instead they decided on the privacy of Jake's place.

Paige sat quietly while Jake built a fire. She gazed up at the pitched, wood beam ceiling and admired the sense of space it created. Looking around, she could see the room was furnished comfortably in earth tones, with brown leather chairs and western style lamps made of sculpted metal and antlers. A cowhide rug covered the wood floor in front of the fireplace.

Jake placed a wire screen in front of the fire as it began to catch, small flames growing into larger ones. He placed a bottle of brandy on the pine table in front of the couch and poured a serving for each of them. She took the snifter he handed to her and then sat back on the couch, waiting apprehensively for the conversation to unfold.

Jake sat on the rug, looking into the fire. He avoided Paige's inquiring gaze as he worked to pull his thoughts together. He took a sip of the brandy, swirling it around the glass, just as he'd done with his coffee the first time Paige had seen him. Then slowly he started to let the story flow. As nervous as he felt about their safety, they were both already involved, whether they wanted to be or not. And it felt good to share the tale he had carried alone for so long.

"I grew up with the legend," Jake explained. "My grandfather was an odd man, very back woods and more than a little eccentric. He told many tales of the old west, some believable and some pretty farfetched." Jake paused to take another sip of brandy and then continued on as Paige took a warming sip from her own snifter.

"Most people thought he was crazy when he told his story about hidden gold. For one thing, he just didn't come across as very believable, what with all the wild tales he was always telling. For another, the story seemed too unlikely. After all, historical accounts state that the early prospectors and miners were unsuccessful in their attempts to find gold in Jackson Hole. One man, after years of searching, left only the equivalent of twelve dollars behind in his cabin when he passed away. So, it just didn't sound likely that anyone could have found a large amount." Jake paused to raise the brandy snifter to his mouth again and then placed it on the table, throwing a sideways glance at Paige.

"But I knew, even as a child, that he was telling the truth. I've always had a good instinct about things and I knew this was one story I could believe in." This time Jake paused without taking a drink, instead just looking into the fire and then turning to face Paige directly.

"According to the way he told it, his father – that would be my great-grandfather - and a friend had been panning for gold along the Snake River, just as many had been doing in those days. No one around them had come up with anything more than a few tiny bits of gold and slowly, one by one, they had given up, believing there wasn't any more to be found.

But my great-grandfather and his friend moved a little ways downstream and gave one more area alongside the river a few tries. To their shock, they began to dig up larger chunks of ore. They hid the pieces and decided to come back later, when no one else would be around to observe them."

At this point Jake stopped and stood up, left the room and came back with a standard map of the valley of Jackson Hole. He moved a few books out of the way, set his brandy snifter to the side and laid the map open across the table. Here he pointed to the path of the Snake River, how it wound its way through the valley, meandering as it continued south. He pointed a finger to an area not far from Deadman's Bar, indicating this as the approximate location that his great grandfather and friend had found the gold ore while panning that day.

"They went back that night," he continued, "with a lantern and pitchforks and a couple of small potato sacks. They dug most of the night, finding nothing as the hours passed by. Discouraged, they came close to giving up. But shortly before the sun rose, my great- grandfather dug up a nugget the size of his fist. Hardly believing his eyes, he continued digging, finding more where that came from. The two men continued digging until the light made it too risky. Not wanting them to be found, they buried their findings and covered the hole, moving brush around to conceal the location."

Paige sat on the couch, nodding her head occasionally and trying to take everything in. On the one hand, it validated everything she had come to suspect, that the early prospectors hadn't been as unsuccessful as history portrayed. On the other hand, however, it was almost unbelievable to hear the tale told as it was. She whispered for Jake to continue and leaned forward to hear the rest.

"They went back every night after that, for weeks," Jake explained. "Each night they dug a little deeper and added more to their stash. Each morning, before the sun rose, they refilled the spot to hide it." Jake tapped his finger against the spot on the map, again indicating where the discovery and subsequent activity had taken place.

"Eventually, as the pieces of gold they were finding became smaller and smaller, they determined they had exhausted the lode. They covered the area one final time and returned to my great grandfather's cabin to decide on a course of action."

Here Jake paused and stared into the fire, considering the story from a few different angles. No matter how many ways he had looked at the overall picture, there was always more than one possible conclusion. The trick was finding the one that was right.

"From what I was told as a boy," Jake now explained, "they decided that my great grandfather's friend would hide it – for what reason I never really understood – and that he'd make a map of the location, which would be copied and kept by each of them, under an honor system. My great grandfather believed that his friend kept the gold hidden in his cellar for a few years and then buried it somewhere in the mountains. They were to meet together to discuss the location of the buried gold. But before he could tell my great grandfather where he had buried it, he was swept away in the great Kelly flood of 1927. He drowned, leaving no trace of the gold behind."

"I remember reading about that," Paige spoke up, recalling some of the initial research she had done on the area. "A natural dam had been formed by a landslide two years earlier and heavy rain and snowmelt caused it to collapse."

"Exactly," Jake nodded in agreement. "That was the Gros Ventre Slide in 1925 that formed the natural dam. It was also caused by heavy rain and snowmelt. Fifty million cubic feet of rock slid off Sheep Mountain, up behind Kelly. Created a rock wall two hundred feet high. Pretty much wiped out the whole town."

Paige continued to take all of this in. She leaned forward to look at the map carefully, trying to imagine how they could possibly search the entire valley. It could take years, generations, even. At this point, it seemed like an impossible task. She began to feel a little sorry for Jake, pursuing a dream that wasn't likely to be realized.

"So you really have no idea where the gold could be," Paige asked in a sympathetic tone.

Jake sat quietly for a minute, which Paige interpreted as agreement. She watched Jake as he stared ahead into the fire. And she watched as he stood up and crossed the room to a tall bookshelf against the front wall. He hesitated briefly and then reached up to one of the upper rows and pulled out one of the books. Flipping through the pages, he removed a folded piece of paper and brought it back to where they had been sitting. He sat down again and, holding the paper tightly, looked at Paige.

"I'd been researching the Jackson Hole area most of my life, reading everything I could get my hands on. I analyzed maps, read trail books and studied the local history. But I just couldn't find any leads that seemed strong enough to pursue. Then, about a year ago, I got a call from a man claiming to be the son of my great grandfather's friend. He said that he had some information that would be of interest to me, that it could turn out to be a winning proposition for both of us. I first assumed it was a crank call, but then he threw out a few details that matched the story that I had been told as a boy. The more I listened, the more I became convinced that he was telling the truth."

"I moved down here from Cody about six months ago. It took a little time to sell my property up there and get settled here, but I figured it was my best chance to focus on finding the gold, since I'd been promised the extra information and help. Except for one thing – those promises didn't materialize once I arrived. Instead, Frank - that is, that's who it turned out to be – became very standoffish and seemingly confused about details. He contradicted himself about specifics and was unable to find items that he'd promised to turn over. I spent months running in circles and getting nowhere at all until just recently, when he said he'd found something to give me that would help. As frustrated as I'd become with him, I agreed to meet him and hear what he had to say, which is when he gave me this."

Jake unfolded the paper, which Paige saw was actually two pieces of paper which fit together along a tear down the middle. Looking at the various markings, she could see that it was a map of the valley, though the specific landmarks were not very clear.

"The map must have been already torn when you got it," Paige said, noting the worn edges of the center.

"Actually," Jake said, a slight tone of annoyance in his voice, "the first time I met him he only gave me half of the map, claiming that the other half had been lost. It took a couple meetings and some angry words to get the other half from him. But finally he handed it over."

Paige remembered watching the heated discussion in the town square, as well as seeing the man hand over an envelope. At the time she hadn't realized it was Frank, but now it seemed to be coming together, except for the part about Maddie.

"I don't understand where Maddie fits into all of this," Paige remarked.

"Well, neither do I," Jake sighed. "I didn't even know she was involved until you mentioned it earlier. But obviously they're working together. And from what we just overheard, they're not up to any good."

Paige mulled all this over, trying to put the pieces together. She looked at the map again and then looked up at Jake.

"I don't understand where he got the map," she said.

"He said he's had it for most of his life," Jake answered. "That when his family went through the ruins of his father's house after the flood, they found a water tight box buried beneath the ground. The erosion of the soil had caused the box to become partially unburied, but the box managed to keep the water out. The map was inside and Frank has been searching for the gold ever since. Now that he's too old to continue searching on his own, he offered to split the fortune if I could help find it."

"I see," Paige responded. "That all makes sense, except for the fact that his story doesn't match up with what we overheard. Maddie must have had the map all along and paid Frank, or Lou, or whatever his real name is, to find the treasure for her. So what's the next step?"

"I'm not sure," Jake said honestly. "But we're going to have to find it without them knowing. Somehow we'll need to keep them off track."

Several minutes passed without any conversation at all, at which point Paige turned to Jake suddenly.

"It just occurred to me," she said, "that Maddie has no idea I know anything about this. She simply thinks I'm interested in the history of prospectors and miners in this area, from a comment I made one time at the Blue Sky Café."

Jake waited for Paige to continue, trying to figure out how this could tie in.

"Jake, don't you see?" Paige said. "Since she thinks that I don't know much, I can easily lead them in the wrong direction. I can drop a couple of hints that I've found something for the article I'm doing and make it seem like there may be gold hidden in a different location than it is. I can say I met up with you or that I saw you hiking or something like that, which will throw them off track."

They both thought this over, Jake worrying that it might backfire and put Paige in danger, Paige wondering where she should try to lead them as a decoy location, considering she didn't even know where Jake was looking in the first place.

"Jake," Paige said, "They have no intention of sharing this with you, if it even exists." She quickly retracted her statement as he threw her an annoyed look.

"Ok, I do believe you that it exists. But they have no intention of sharing it. They're just using you. And if Frank's an imposter - which is what it's starting to sound like - the gold is rightfully yours, not his. By the way," she continued, "Do you even have any idea where it's hidden?"

Jake nodded and pointed to an area on the large map, indicating the mountains behind Jenny Lake.

"I'm almost certain it's in this area," he said. "My great grandfather used to go on and on about these mountains, about how his friend always talked about needing to hide it high above the valley. Look at the map here." Jake indicated the smaller, torn map that Frank had given him. "You see these zigzag lines on the left? Those are the Grand Tetons. And the oval shape here...I'm sure that represents Jenny Lake. Now look at the bottom of the paper. You see these parallel lines that look like a ladder or walkway? Or maybe even a bridge? I think that might indicate a crossing point over the Snake River. And the winding line down the middle is the river itself, which points directly towards the Tetons, at least at several of its turns."

Jake stopped to catch his breath and waited for a response from Paige, who sat there quietly analyzing the map herself.

"I don't know, Jake," she replied slowly. "Those are all good guesses, but there are so many possibilities, it's hard to know where to start. There are walkways and bridges and river crossings all over this valley. And ladder markings could represent an actual ladder, which would likely be long gone, or just a directional sign drawn out as a clue."

Paige looked at the map sideways and then turned it in varying directions. Seeing it from different angles, she could see that Jake was right. The zigzag line was almost certainly the Grand Tetons and, if so, the winding line was situated right where the Snake River would be. But that still didn't help. The hiding place could be off in any direction, but pointing that out would serve no purpose other than to discourage Jake. She gathered up as much positive attitude as she could before speaking up.

"So what we need to do is to find the gold first and then lead them to think it's hidden in another area. I think I can help you find it and help you sidetrack them, too."

Jake listened carefully to Paige and nodded slowly in agreement. It was possible the plan could work.

"OK," he said slowly. "We'll start tomorrow morning. I'll give you a ride to your cabin now and I'll pick you up around seven a.m." Just thinking about the early morning start, he found himself stifling a yawn.

"You do know how to make coffee, don't you?" he teased.

Paige laughed and nodded her head. "I make excellent coffee."

Jake looked at Paige, the glow of the fire's embers resting warmly against her face. Impulsively, he leaned over and kissed the side of her cheek.

"I'll bet you do," he said with a smile.

CHAPTER EIGHTEEN

The sun was up long before seven the next morning, but Paige and Jake could hardly tell for all the gray clouds in the sky. A dense layer of fog covered the valley floor, blocking their view of the mountain peaks. The threat of rain weighed heavily in the air. In spite of the less than ideal conditions for heading into the mountains, the situation was starting to feel urgent. They needed to move quickly if they were going to stay a few steps ahead of Frank and Maddie.

Paige was waiting with a full thermos of French Roast when Jake arrived. She twisted the cap off and passed the container under Jake's nose, watching his nod of approval.

"Don't tell me you travel with a coffee grinder," he said with mock surprise, inhaling the aroma of recently ground brew.

"Absolutely," Paige responded, proud to have added a modern touch to the frontier.

Dressed in warm layers of outerwear and wearing sturdy hiking boots, they tossed two lightweight backpacks of supplies in the truck and headed towards Jenny Lake, working their way carefully through the fog. Between them, they were equipped with enough maps, trail mix, flashlights and first aid supplies to cover them for a one day hike. Jake also carried a copy of the map Frank had given him.

"It'll burn off soon," Jake said, watching Paige look out the window and reading her thoughts.

Having already ruled out the lower areas on his previous hike, Jake led Paige quickly along the two mile stretch around the lake and up beyond Hidden Falls. Arriving a half mile later at Inspiration Point, they paused to admire the view. Even misty and gray as it was, there was a dramatic beauty in the view across the valley.

At the Forks of Cascade Canyon, Jake turned left and headed up towards Hurricane Pass, having already covered the right fork on his recent hike to Lake Solitude. By instinct, he led the way while Paige followed along, occasionally stopping to jot down observations. One short section at a time, they climbed higher, noting landmarks along the way.

As they rounded one curve in the trail, a cluster of trees came into view. The trio of tall, mature pines would undoubtedly have been there long before the gold would have been hidden. Behind the trees a concave indentation marked the surface of a wide stretch of rock. From there a cliff shot up several hundred feet in a solid burst of sandstone. Jake paced off the distance between the trail and the grouping of trees and then motioned to Paige to continue on.

Light drops of rain began to fall as they climbed higher and the path soon grew narrow and more difficult to navigate. A steep slab of rock pressed in on them from the right. To their left the ground dropped off abruptly, the roar of Cascade Creek echoing up from below.

This would not be a great place to slip, Paige thought as she took cautious steps forward. Nor would it be a good place to get caught in a rock slide, either, she reasoned, quickening her pace to move ahead to a wider part of the trail.

The rain grew steadier as they continued to document sections of the trail. Even the wildlife seemed to have backed away from the gloomy weather, choosing to stay in burrows or within thickets for protection. Still, Page and Jake pushed on. At one point, Paige stepped too quickly over a fallen rock, slipping sideways with her foot. She barely caught her balance in time to keep from falling.

"Maybe we should turn around," Jake offered, growing concerned. "We could come back out tomorrow when the weather should be better."

Paige motioned for him to push ahead, but within seconds the rain started to pound down with a fury. Jake turned around and shook his head. A heavy gust of wind blew across the canyon, whipping falling leaves up against the side of his face.

"It's too dangerous to keep going," Jake shouted over the storm's wailing. "We're going to have to wait this out."

Reaching out to Paige, he grabbed her hand tightly, pulling her along as he pushed his way through thick brush on the trail's cliff-side edge. Emerging on the other side of the tangled branches, he pulled her into a narrow hollow within the rocky surface of the cliff, where they hovered beneath an overhang. Though the space was cold and isolated, most of the rain was blocked.

"Well, one thing is for sure," Paige commented, wrapping her arms across her chest in an attempt to keep warm. "Old Man Thompson would never be able to hike up this far, not anymore."

"Exactly why he gave in and asked me to help," Jake said, nodding his head in agreement.

"I suspect he never intended to share anything with you," Paige sighed, pulling the collar of her jacket closer to her chin. "If it's even his to share, that is. Which I seriously doubt at this point."

"Or he may have intended to share it originally and just got greedy along the way," Jake offered, watching the rain continue to pour down.

Paige cast a quick glance at Jake, fighting back a smile at his half-sweet, half-naïve stance. "You're a good guy, Jake. You give him more credit than I would."

Jake laughed, understanding the complimentary jab Paige had just delivered.

"I guess I just like to believe people are trustworthy," he replied. "You know, innocent until proven guilty. Give people the benefit of the doubt."

"You wouldn't last long in New York City, I'm afraid," Paige laughed.

"I'm not sure I'd want to," Jake tossed back. "I've never been there, but I have the impression that it's a whole different planet."

"That may be the understatement of the century," Paige agreed, contemplating their current trailside predicament. It was a far cry from that of rain-soaked Manhattan city-dwellers attempting to hail cabs from curbs.

"So, getting back to your situation with Frank," Paige continued, "Who knows what his original plan was? Or if it was even his plan at all, considering Maddie is somehow mixed up in all this. Whatever the case may be, it's a betrayal, whether he – or they – originally intended to include you or not."

Unrelenting, the downpour continued full-force for another twenty minutes before it finally started to ease up. Once it was feasible to tackle the trail again, they stepped cautiously away from the security of the overhang. Slowly, they descended the canyon, ultimately arriving back at the lake's western edge. Though exhausted and drenched, they nearly ran the last two miles around the lake to get back to the dry, warmth of the truck.

* * * *

"There are three places along that trail that I think might be hiding the gold," Jake said over the steam rising from his mug. He and Paige sat in front of the fire at the ranch house, hot cocoa helping them recover from the stormy hike.

"One must be that tall cluster of trees that was off to the side near the indented rock formation," Paige ventured, remembering how much time he had spent taking notes in that area.

Jake nodded his head in agreement. "Yes, that's one, though there's another location that looks very similar on the Lake Solitude trail, which we didn't take today. A second possibility from today's search was the area where the trail suddenly widened after that very narrow section."

"But you barely stopped there," Paige pointed out.

"I know," Jake agreed, with a clear tone of frustration. "The weather was too unpredictable. I knew we couldn't stop and take notes the entire way."

She thought this over for a minute and then asked Jake where the third area was.

Jake pulled out the large map and placed the smaller, handmade map on top of it. He pointed to the actual split of the Forks itself. Paige peered up at him with a questioning look. He pointed back to the map again.

"There's another cluster of trees about here, up away from the trail about twelve paces or so. I noticed it the last time I hiked up there." Jake spoke as if talking to himself, but Paige was following along and thinking of the pacing he had done at other points along the trail.

"Why that particular spot?" she asked, confused.

"Look here," Jake said, pointing to the bottom of the map Frank had given him. "The lines that look like a ladder or bridge, I think they may be tallies of paces. The trio of arrows to the right could indicate a formation of three trees. They would have to be tall ones to have been there since then. And the semi-circle beyond that must indicate the shape of some sort of boulder or something. I think we're looking for a combination of all those factors."

Paige looked over the markings at the bottom of the map again. It was true that they could be interpreted the way Jake described, but it still seemed he was grasping.

"I don't know, Jake," Paige said, reluctant to dampen his enthusiasm. "I don't want to discourage you, but it still seems the clues are too general. And those ladder markers, if that's what they are, aren't close enough to the trio marks."

Jake shook his head with the determined look common when someone does not want to be dissuaded.

"Look, I not only have this map to go by, but also the descriptions I've heard since I was a boy – that the gold would be hidden high above the valley floor, that it was tucked away below some sort of rock formation and that it could be found by following water. These are the descriptions that Jeremiah himself passed on, those given to him by his friend. He explained them in detail to my grandfather, who told me the same details over and over…" He stopped short, puzzled at the expression that had come over Paige.

"Did you say Jeremiah?" she asked, her eyes widening.

Jake looked at her with confusion. "Yeah, Jeremiah Norris, my great grandfather. Why?"

A strange look came over Paige's face, one that he'd never seen on her before. To Jake's surprise, Paige put down her mug of cocoa suddenly, sending a small, chocolate wave splattering over the edge. She jumped to her feet and grabbed her jacket.

"I need you to take me home," she said quickly, already walking toward the door. She motioned to Jake to hurry up. "Just take me home to get my car and I'll catch up with you later."

"But, Paige…," he started to respond, confused by her quick change in demeanor.

"I think I can help you with this." Paige opened the front door abruptly, causing it to slam inward. She ignored the sharp sound of the door's contact with the wall and started across the porch.

"Alright, I'll help, too," Jake offered, jumping up quickly.

"No, I'm afraid that won't work," Paige tossed over her shoulder while continuing to walk. "There's somewhere I need to go."

"Then I'll go with you," Jake called after her, grabbing his keys and a jacket.

"You can't," Paige answered brusquely, whipping around quickly to face him. "I mean…I mean, you have to trust me on this."

Jake pushed for an explanation a few more times, but to no avail. When he saw that she was determined to head out on her own, he reluctantly gave up. Whatever arguing he might continue to do, it would be wasted energy. He started up the truck and, at Paige's insistence, drove as quickly as possible, dropping her off at her cabin.

"I haven't the least idea what you're doing, but be careful," he called as she jumped into her car and started it up.

Paige waved in a rushed manner, pulling out on the road and heading quickly towards town. Please, she thought to herself, please let this work.

The roads were slick from the rain, which had started to fall in torrents again. She flipped her windshield wipers on low, but immediately switched them to the highest setting. Water-filled potholes sent deep-toned splashes against the underside of her vehicle. Gripping the steering wheel tightly, she scanned the sides of the road for elk and bison, hoping to avoid a collision if one unexpectedly started to cross the roadway.

In spite of the weather-hindered roads, she made the drive in record time and grabbed the first parking space she saw, about a block from the center of town. Walking quickly, but being cautious to avoid drawing attention to herself, she made her way to the town square.

The gray of the antler arch was dull and dark in the falling rain. Very few people wandered along the edge of the square. A woman in her mid-thirties walked a golden retriever, one hand holding its leash, the other clutching the chin straps of a slick rain hood. A man stood under the covering of the local bus stop, a newspaper braced above his head for additional shelter from the rain. Three teenage boys horsed around on the opposite side of the square, oblivious to the spatters of mud and splashes of water that their shenanigans sent flying. Twilight was fast approaching and the neon light of The Million Dollar Cowboy Bar glowed in the background, gleams of colored light oozing out into the wet, misty air.

Paige looked around slowly and then returned her gaze to focus on the antler arch again. Closing her eyes, she summoned up all the energy she could. It had to work, she thought. She knew this was the best chance to help Jake. She stood for what seemed like a very long time, listening in turn to the splashing of vehicles passing by on the rain-slicked roads, the carefree laughter of the boys across the square and the air-pressured brakes of the local bus stopping to pick up its passenger.

Slowly, however, the sounds faded away into mere background noise and, soon after that, into silence. A sense of peaceful relaxation washed over her. She opened her eyes and looked up, finding that her hopes had paid off. The top of the antler arch had just a faint glow to it. Paige stepped forward and searched the ground, but there was no sign of the skeleton key. She paced several yards to each side of the arch, but the sidewalk was clear of debris. Sticking one boot into a large puddle, she tapped the pavement, searching for any object the water might be hiding, but there was nothing. Just as she was starting to fear that she'd have to give up, she spotted a small scrap of silver sticking out from a shrub on the other side of the arch. From the dull tone of the metal and the smooth curve of the upper edge, she recognized it as the top of the key. She looked around, took a deep breath and stepped through the arch.

CHAPTER NINETEEN

The smell of fresh hay and the sound of neighing horses filled the late afternoon air. Thin rays of light filtered through the roof, casting a golden glow on the ground and against the walls of the livery barn. Paige looked around, first to the right, out the front barn door, where two cowboys sauntered by on horses, and then out the back door, where she saw nothing but open space and mountains. Looking down, she found herself wearing an old, baggy pair of blue overalls, an even baggier white shirt and brown work boots. Lifting her hands to her head, she felt the rough leather of a hat, as well as the width of a wide brim encircling the hat itself. Her hands moved down to her shoulders, where she felt the texture of her hair. Impulsively, she gathered the hair into her hands and tucked it up underneath her hat.

Walking over to the back door, she looked out across the open field, but saw no activity, other than a few chickens pecking at the ground. She peered around the side of the barn, finding the small wagon she remembered parked against the wall. At the unexpected sound of a horse stomping its hoof inside the barn, she pulled back inside a little too quickly, knocking a horse shoe off the wall, which fell against a flat, metal trough of water and sent a clattering echo into the rafters. Now, even more startled, she leaned against a wood beam until her heart stopped racing, only to soon find herself jumping again.

"Can I help ya, young fella?" a man's voice called from the front barn door. Paige looked across the expansive interior of the barn and squinted to see where the voice was coming from, but the sun had lowered in the sky and now was shining directly in her eyes.

"I said hello," the voice said, a little louder this time. "Is there anything I can do fer ya?" Paige felt at a loss for words, but somehow pulled herself together when the figure came close enough for her to recognize Chester standing in front of her. At this point, he narrowed his eyes and took a good look at her, lifted his hand to his chin and rubbed it back and forth. Paige decided she had to say something and took the chance of speaking up.

"Chester, it's me," she said cautiously, watching Chester continue to squint and stare, clearly confused.

Not intending to cause him additional confusion, but in an attempt to clarify, Paige slowly lifted one hand to her head and pulled the hat off to the side, her soft, auburn hair falling down across her shoulders.

Chester's eyes popped wide open and blinked several times. He opened his mouth to say something and then closed it again without a word. He repeated this sequence again, still not finding any words. Finally he gave up and just stood there, staring.

"Chester, I'm sorry, I didn't mean to scare you," Paige said tentatively. "It's me, Pai...er...I mean Maylene." She held her breath, waiting for his response.

"I know who you are," Chester said, his eyes wide as saucers. "I just can't figure out what you're doing in that get up there." His eyes looked her up and down as he shook his head in disbelief. "And where've you been, anyway? Haven't seen you around since that ride we took, up on the butte."

"Well, I've been…I've been…" Paige attempted to answer, but knew there wasn't a good explanation, at least not a believable one.   She paused and decided to change the direction of the conversation.

"Chester, I may need your help," Paige said. "There are a lot of things I'm not going to be able to explain, but I'm probably going to need someone's help and you're the only one I feel I can trust." Paige paused, watching Chester and waiting for a reaction.

"You're sure a funny one, ma'am, if I do say so myself. Never met one quite like you," Chester sighed. "But if I can help you, I surely will. You just tell me what you need and I'll do anything I can."

Paige quickly put the wide brimmed hat back on her head, tucking her hair underneath it again. She pulled the hat down and checked around her neck for any loose strands of hair. Satisfied there weren't any showing, she shook her overalls and shirt to make sure they were hanging as baggily as they could and then looked up at Chester.

"Well, the first thing you can do is tell me if I look like a guy," Paige asked.

"I sure ain't never seen a lady dressed like that, if that's what you mean, ma'am, and I don't mean any offence by saying that, you understand." Chester tried to choose his words carefully, not wanting to say anything that might be taken as an insult, but seeing that Paige was desperately waiting for an answer.

"Chester, if you saw me walking down the street like this, would you think I might possibly be a woman?" Again, Paige waited expectantly for his response.

"No, ma'am, I certainly wouldn't," Chester answered honestly, hoping for his own sake that this was the answer she was looking for.

Paige looked relieved and then pushed for a little more clarification.

"So if you saw me sitting in the saloon, looking like this, you wouldn't think I was a woman?"

"No, I wouldn't, ma'am. We don't expect to see women in the saloon in the first place, so I don't think the idea would even occur to anyone in there. You wouldn't be recognized. Not dressed like that, you wouldn't." Chester stood back and looked at her carefully. "No, you'd be alright. You got a young face and you ain't wearing any of that fancy paint that some of them women do. They'd just take you fer a young man, that's what they'd do." Chester paused before quickly adding "Again, I sure don't mean any offence by that, ma'am."

It was exactly what Paige wanted to hear. Checking to make sure Chester would be around later, she adjusted her hat one more time, stepped out the front door of the livery and walked calmly down the street, assuming a leisurely but confident stride, as she figured a man might do.

Tuttle's Saloon was crowded, as crowded as a place can be in a barely established town. The bar was lined with men of varying heights and dress, most wearing hats and engaged in animated conversations with neighbors on adjacent bar stools. It was not difficult for Paige to slip in essentially unnoticed, where she took one of the few empty seats, this one at the end of the bar.

Around her, the level of activity swirled with high energy. Four men – the same four men she had seen before, from what Paige could tell – were carrying on an animated card game in the corner, setting aside their poker faces in order to have a dispute of some sort. One man paced the floor with a glass of whiskey in his hand. Two women in tight, gaudy attire leaned seductively against the far end of the bar – ladies of the night, Paige surmised by their high cut hemlines and even lower cut necklines, or even possibly dance hall girls from The Clubhouse. This clearly worked in her favor, as the attention of the men not otherwise engaged in drinking or arguing seemed to be directed toward the two women.

There was no sign of Jeremiah, to Paige's disappointment. But at the moment it was Cyrus she hoped to see and in this wish she found herself lucky, as he was sitting just two seats away from her at the bar. He appeared restless and nervous, fidgeting with his glass frequently. Between gulps of whiskey, he tapped his fingers against the wood grain of the bar's counter top. Every now and then he glanced over his shoulder and then turned back to his whiskey again.

"What'll you be drinkin' today, young fella?" The bartender's voice startled Paige out of her observation of the bar and its various customers. Looking up cautiously, she was relieved to find the majority of the bartender's attention was focused on a glass he was drying.

"A whiskey," Paige muttered, keeping her voice as low as she could without sounding unnatural. She watched as the bartender sauntered over to a row of bottles, picked out one that was almost full and poured a short glass half-way to the top.

As he approached the bar area in front of her seat, a new panic gripped Paige. It was doubtful she had any money. These get-ups that she kept finding herself in were designed more for fitting in with the surroundings than for actual day-to-day living.

"This one's on the house," the bartender said as he slid the glass casually down the counter. "A young man passing through Jackson ought to be allowed a welcome drink."

Paige breathed a sigh of relief. Just as it had been when Chester had taken her to the top of the butte in the wagon, she was off the hook monetarily.

Cyrus continued to look around between swallows of his drink. It was clear he was watching the door and waiting for someone. With each passing minute he grew more impatient. Paige guessed that the person he was waiting for was late, which would explain his continuous glances toward the entrance of the saloon. Or, on the other hand, he might just be nervous. This would be merited, she thought, if her suspicions were correct.

Paige took a sip of her drink, not wanting to appear too conspicuous by not touching it. The rough liquid burned as it slid down her throat and she had to hold back to keep from choking. She had always favored a nice merlot or chardonnay over liquor and she knew the abrasive liquid in her glass was a far cry from the products of modern day distilleries.

As Paige was attempting to get a second taste of the hideous drink across her lips, she noticed a woman enter the saloon, making a snake-like entrance in a rich, plum-colored velvet dress. The plunging neckline and sleeves were trimmed with ruffled layers of rose lace. Tiny pearls dotted the seams along the back of the sleeves, catching the bar's light and twinkling in a star-like fashion. Her dark brown hair was partially swept up under a velvet hat of the same color, edged in matching, glistening pearls and tilted slightly over her forehead. The rest tumbled down over her shoulders in wild ringlets of curls.

She made her way across the room, ignoring the stares of a few of the men, and placed herself firmly against the bar to one side of Cyrus, who looked up at her with an expression that was a mixture of hunger and fear. Leaning towards him in a sultry fashion, she rested her hand on his shoulder and appeared to whisper something in his ear. These hushed words triggered a wide smile across his face and a twinkling in his eyes that appeared almost boyish in the glow of the lantern-lit saloon.

"Well now, don't you look mighty fine tonight, Ruby." Cyrus spoke with the cockiness of a man trying to impress. "That velvet sure does light up your pretty face."

"Now, Cyrus, that's about the nicest thing you could say to a lady and I do thank you," the woman responded in a sweet, sugary tone. She nodded yes to the bartender's silent offer of a drink.

"Ain't tellin' you nothin' but the truth," Cyrus added with a school-boy grin. "Why, Ruby, as sure as these mountains are high, you're the prettiest female to ever set foot in this valley. And I've seen a few come through before, but none as fine as you."

Again, the woman leaned over and whispered in Cyrus' ear. And again he blushed and fumbled nervously with his drink. They continued in this manner for some time, exchanging whispered conversation as Cyrus seemed to melt little by little into the bar counter.

With the continuing rain and approach of evening hours, the saloon became more crowded. A few men hovered around the bar, while others stood alone or in groups in the center of the room. Others rested against the wall next to Paige, oblivious to her, yet making her nervous, nonetheless. She didn't need one of them accidentally bumping into her and knocking her hat to the floor. Seizing a sudden opportunity to grab a seat that emptied next to the lady in velvet, she moved into a better spot from which to try to overhear Cyrus' conversation. With the woman leaning against the bar, blocking his view, her move to the closer bar stool was not noticed. She positioned her back away from them and took another burning sip of the whiskey, adjusting her hat forward a little, partially to hide her face and partially to conceal her grimace as she tried to swallow.

The noise level increased as the saloon filled and escalated even more as the customers filled themselves with spirits. Conversation became looser and, while many paid little attention to what others were saying, Paige listened more carefully, especially to the words being exchanged next to her. The efforts paid off, as phrases began to drift over to her.

"It's not going to be easy in this rain," Cyrus was heard saying.

"Well, a little water ain't gonna hurt you," the woman laughed nonchalantly. "You can do this for me, can't ya, Cyrus, sweetie? For us?" Her voice sounded as sweet and sticky as honey as it floated across Paige's back and reached her ears. Had she been able to look behind her, she was sure she would have seen the woman stroke Cyrus' cheek as she oozed these words at him. Even without seeing it, his reaction to Ruby's lavish flattery was clear. He would do anything she asked.

Cyrus called to the bartender for another round of drinks for himself and the lady. As the conversation evolved, it was clear a plan was being formed. "Yes, tonight...as soon as it's dark enough...quite a distance...hide it well...saddle up...he won't be able to find it, don't worry" were portions of the conversation that Paige was able to make out.

She lingered, but was unable to pick up any more information as the din of the bar activity continued to rise. Knowing she needed to act quickly, Paige slipped out the door and hurried back to the livery stable, where she found Chester tending the horses, as she knew she would. She looked around for any sign of Jeremiah, but it was clear that Chester was the only one there.

"Chester, I need your help," Paige said, slightly out of breath from her brisk walk from the saloon.

"No problem," Chester replied. "You just tell me what you need. Your wish is my command, as they say." He made a noise that sounded like a sigh and laugh mixed together, a sign of resignation. His encounters with Paige were just destined to be a little out of the ordinary.

"This is going to sound odd," Paige warned him, as he brushed down a sturdy, golden work horse. "But I'm going to need to follow someone tonight, and I don't think a wagon is going to work. I was planning to follow on foot, but I overheard the words 'saddle up' so I have a feeling it may be too far to walk."

"Do you have any idea where you're going to end up?" Chester asked.

"No," Paige said hesitantly.

"So you don't know how far it is?" Chester continued, giving Paige a puzzled look.

"No," Paige said with a sigh.

"And the people we're following said something about saddling up?" Chester asked, to make sure he had the facts straight, what few there were.

"Yes, I'm sure I heard that," Paige answered.

Chester thought over this information and then summed it up on his own.

"So we need to follow someone or some people somewhere, possibly nearby, possibly not, and you believe this person or these people will be traveling by horse?"

"Yes, that's about all I know," Paige answered meekly.

Chester shook his head, half humored and half amazed that he was about to agree to such a crazy scheme, but he knew he was going to say yes before she even explained. There wasn't much to go on, but at least he could try to help.

"OK," Chester said. "We'll saddle up two horses. I'll take my usual horse, Fire, and you take Cinnamon, who's always good about behaving with strangers. Whoever we're following will probably take a lantern. In order for our horses to not be heard, we'll need to follow the light, rather than following their horses directly. And we can't stay close to them or they'll catch on that they're being followed. We can't take a lantern ourselves without being seen. It'll be tricky, but we'll try."

"That sounds like it could work," Paige agreed, thinking this over. Suddenly the fleeting thought hit her that it had been years since she had been on a horse. She figured it might be wise to warn Chester.

"I haven't been on a horse for a long time, Chester, but I'll do my best," she said as casually as possible, hoping it wouldn't cause him to back off from the whole plan.

At this comment, Chester gave her a puzzled look. "Excuse me for asking, ma'am, but if you ain't been on a horse for a long time, how do you get around to places you need to go?"

"Well, I…" Paige said hesitantly, "That would be a little hard to explain." She saw the bewildered look in Chester's face and decided it would be best to move on quickly.

"I don't think we have much time," Paige said anxiously, looking out the barn door and seeing that it was almost dark. Chester nodded, quickly bringing Fire and Cinnamon around to the center of the barn and saddling them up. Mounting his horse with ease, he motioned for Paige to do the same.

Paige stared at the horse, the saddle and the stirrup. Memories of riding when she was younger came vaguely back to her, but she was reminded now that not only had it been a long time, but it had been a good twenty years. The last time she'd been riding was at a summer camp she'd attended as a teen. Inserting her foot into the stirrup, she tried to push up and swing her leg over Cinnamon, who was patiently eyeing her from a slightly turned head. Failing the first time, she placed her free foot back down on the ground and gave it a second try. This time she succeeded, though it took her a minute to get adjusted into the saddle. She could almost swear that both Chester and Cinnamon were silently laughing, but she shook this off, being close to laughing herself.

Riding quietly out the back door of the livery stable, Chester helped guide Paige to a shed not far from Tuttle's, which was close enough to watch customers departing, yet hidden enough to keep out of sight. Their timing was lucky, as it wasn't long before Cyrus emerged from the saloon. He was followed by the woman who had been leaning next to him at the bar. He wrapped a possessive arm around her, which she shook off after a moment, pointing toward the mountains.

"Ma'am," Chester said a touch of nervousness in his voice. "Is that who you're figurin' to follow, Cyrus Thompson? 'Cuz he ain't no one to mess with. That man's as mean as a snake"

Paige took little heed in Chester's hesitation. At this point, she was determined to follow this through, regardless of the risk.

"We'll just have to be careful," she said firmly. Chester sighed, but Paige knew he would go along with the plan at this point, however crazy it might be.

They watched while Cyrus untied a horse from a post in front of the saloon. He jumped on quickly, snapped his reins and set off toward the east. Keeping a safe distance, Paige and Chester followed carefully. Not far from the center of town, Cyrus paused and dismounted his horse, disappearing for a few minutes inside an abandoned shack. When he emerged he held a bulky sack and a dim lantern. He stuffed the sack in a saddlebag and then climbed back on his horse, holding the lantern in his right hand. From there, he continued to the east.

Darkness had almost fallen completely and the moon was covered by clouds. While this made it less likely that they would be seen, it also made it more difficult to ride. Without the lantern Cyrus was carrying up ahead, it would have been impossible. As it was, it wasn't going to be easy. But, cautiously, Chester led the way. Paige followed along, stopping whenever Chester paused and moving ahead slowly when he resumed.

When Cyrus reached the edge of town, he veered to the left and picked up a narrow trail alongside the mountains to the east. The glow of the lantern grew faint as the distance between them stretched out. But Chester held back, not willing to take any chances. It would be better to lose Cyrus than to fall into a confrontation with him, as much as it would have disappointed Paige.

Paige followed along, trying to keep a good sense of direction. It would be crucial for her to be able to remember the entire route later on. She knew she would need to find it again on her own before getting her hands on the skeleton key the next time. And yet again, after she did.

The dark of night masked most of the surroundings, but every now and then a shadowy mass appeared with enough of a silhouette to be identified - a grouping of trees, a heavy wooden fence or small sheds for storing grains. Paige made note of every one of these, tucking the information away for future use.

Eventually their path began to climb, gradually growing steeper. The flat surface of the trail became increasingly rocky. Chester slowed down, becoming more cautious with the horses. They continued in this manner until Chester finally stopped altogether.

"I know this section of the mountain, ma'am. Been up here many a time," he whispered to Paige with a concerned sound in his voice. "It's gonna get mighty steep and too rough for the horses to handle. Our only chance now is to tie them up somewhere and try to go the rest of the way on foot."

"But we'll lose him, won't we?" Paige whispered back.

If Paige could have seen in the dark, she would have noticed that Chester was shaking his head. "I don't think so. It's pretty unlikely that he can do this next part on his horse, either. I think we'll find he's set aside his horse to wait for him, too. We'll still have an equal footing."

Paige climbed down and handed the reins over to Chester, who took the two horses off to the side, tying them securely to a tree. Continuing on foot, Paige could now feel that the ground had grown extremely rough and uneven. Small rocks dug into her feet and the incline of the terrain became more and more severe as they pushed forward. She was tempted a few times to give up and turn around, as the light from the lantern Cyrus carried could barely be seen. But, quite sure that this was her only chance of getting Jake the information he needed, she continued on. Just as Chester had suspected, they soon passed Cyrus' horse.

As the grade of the slope increased, it became necessary to use their hands to balance against boulders and trees.

Occasionally a small rock would become dislodged and tumble to the ground, causing both Paige and Chester to freeze in place, hoping Cyrus would not suspect he was being followed. Yet, it was not uncommon to hear rocks falling and twigs snapping while out hiking, due to the abundance of wildlife activity. A few minor sounds would go unnoticed.

For the better part of two hours, they continued to climb, until Paige felt a weariness in her legs that was so intense she wondered if she could go on. It was just about this time that the dim light of the lantern ahead stopped moving forward. Paige leaned against a sturdy tree, looking around at the surrounding landscape. She could see the shadowy outlines of two other trees just a few yards away. Behind her a boulder stood approximately as high as her shoulder. Other than that, only darkness stretched out in every direction.

"Chester," Paige whispered, unable to see through the depth of night.

The answer came from a few feet away. "Right here, ma'am," Chester replied.

"Where are we?" Paige whispered again.

Chester was quiet for a moment, analyzing the distance they'd covered. "We must be close to the top," he said. "For one thing, look how much higher Cyrus' lantern appears, even though it's not that far away. And it's mighty steep here too, so I think we're probably near the end of the trail." Chester was quiet once again, considering all this before continuing. "If I'm right about this, and I think I am, there's nothing but sheer rock up ahead. He'd have to stop about now."

Paige and Chester lingered in the dark, standing motionless between the trees and boulder. It wasn't long before the sharp sound of metal against rock came down from the direction of the lantern, tentative at first but growing progressively louder as time went on. The strong, repetitive motions echoed through the night with regular precision. As the activity continued, Paige knew the alternating sounds of scraping and falling rocks were what she had hoped to hear.

In time, the sounds ceased. Paige wasn't sure how long they had been waiting quietly in the same spot, but finally it became clear that the lantern was beginning to move again. Chester grabbed Paige's elbow and pulled gently, indicated that they needed to start back.

Quickly they retraced their steps. From above, they could hear sounds of small rocks falling and branches breaking, which helped hide similar sounds they made themselves. Heading downhill was difficult in its own way, as gravity and loose rocks taunted them with potential falls. They made good time, gaining some distance in front of the lantern's light, which continued to follow behind them.

They passed Cyrus' horse as quietly as possible, though it still let out a small whinnying sound, something that could have been made as a reaction to any small animal passing by. Reaching their own horses, they untied them quickly and pulled them back onto the trail, riding in hushed darkness until they emerged in the flatland near town. Ducking out of sight behind a small shed, they waited for Cyrus to pass by. Once he was far enough ahead that they could ride without fear of being heard, they mounted the horses again and rode around the back side of the sleeping town, finally reaching the barn.

"I can't thank you enough," Paige said to Chester once they had the horses put away in their stalls. Chester just shook his head and threw an amused glance in her direction.

"It's no problem, ma'am," he said, a trace of laughter in his voice. "I don't mind. Life sure ain't boring when you're around. A little excitement is welcome anytime in this old barn."

"Where're you stayin', by the way?" Chester asked. "I don't want to leave you out here alone in the dark."

Paige had to think quickly before replying. She thumbed through mental images of the buildings she'd seen when she had first stumbled through the arch. The fledgling town bore little resemblance to modern-day Jackson.

"I've got a room at the Jackson Hotel," she said, remembering the lodging establishment not far from The Clubhouse. "And a key to my room," she added rapidly, "so it won't be any trouble to just slip in. I'll walk over there myself. It's only a short distance. You go on home, Chester, you must be exhausted."

"I have to admit my bones are feelin' weary," Chester agreed. "But I'm mighty pleased to have been of help to you." Had she been able to see in the dark, she would have caught the slight blush that crept onto Chester's face as she leaned over and placed a friendly kiss on his cheek.

Together they pulled the barn door closed and walked out to the roadway. Paige again took notice of the surrounding, empty land, the absence of street lights and the dust below her feet. It was a stark contrast to the scene that would evolve over time.

"You have a good night, now, ma'am," Chester said, as he and Paige parted ways and headed in opposite directions.

Paige walked slowly toward the hotel, gradually taking smaller steps and glancing behind her down the road. As soon as Chester disappeared from sight, Paige turned back, returning quickly to the barn and slipping inside.

She had hoped that Jeremiah would be there when she and Chester returned from the trip up the mountain, though at such a late hour she had known the chance of seeing him was slim.   Just as there had been no sign of him that afternoon, there was no sign of him now. Crouching down, she searched the hay-covered floor for the skeleton key and then checked the walls for hooks or shelves where it might be, but found nothing.

She walked to the door of the barn and glanced up and down the road. The town was still and quiet. Lanterns had long been extinguished and only silence hovered over the old western buildings. Feeling exhaustion creep in, she stepped back into the barn, pulled a horse blanket off of a wooden railing and curled up on a stack of hay in an empty stall. To the soft breathing of Cinnamon, Fire and the other horses, she fell asleep.

CHAPTER TWENTY

Jake paced back and forth across the front room of his ranch house. The sun had been up for an hour already, enough time for him to drive to Paige's cabin and back twice. He was discouraged and more than a little nervous. It hadn't worried him that she was away for the evening. But when the midnight hour rolled around and she still wasn't anywhere to be found, he started to grow increasingly concerned.

He'd slept fitfully and sporadically, waking often and walking to the front door to look around. Each time he hoped to see her car in the driveway, but each time he gazed out it only raised his level of anxiety. There was no sign of her anywhere.

After a restless night of failed attempts at sleep he skipped both coffee and breakfast. He'd had no appetite when he first awakened and, in several hours of being awake, this hadn't changed. Tearing his jacket off the hook in the entry way, he jumped in his truck and headed quickly into town. Still early, the town square was deserted. Early morning light was just settling against the lush green pines of Snow King's slopes. The rain from the day before had let up.

Out of habit, he parked near the Blue Sky Café, but didn't go in. He had no desire for coffee and even less for the idea of facing Maddie and Frank. Instead he walked to the center of town and circled around, heading up and down side streets until he found Paige's car parked half a block from the town square. The sight of frost on the windshield only made him more concerned. It was clear the car had been there all night, but there was no sign anywhere of Paige.

Trying the door on the driver's side, he found it locked. He cupped his hands and peered through the window. Nothing seemed to be amiss. There were a few books scattered on the back seat and a brown, portable, accordion-type file folder resting on the front passenger seat. He circled the car and tried the other door, feeling the cold of the metal handle against his skin. To his relief, the door was unlocked. He pulled it open and picked up the folder. Feeling like an intruder, but weighing his concern for Paige's safety as a priority, he lifted the folding cover and looked inside.

There were several compartments, each with a plastic tab sticking up and a white paper tag inside to identify general contents. One held maps of the area, several marked with various notations, but none of much importance. A second compartment held sheets of paper, all containing historical information about Jackson Hole. The notes were organized in chronological order, starting with accounts of homesteading during the 1800's and continuing on into the development of Jackson as a town. The early post offices of the area were listed. Dates that indicated when prominent buildings were established followed that. Well-known figures in the town's history were also listed, along with characters less known. As the papers continued, a large amount of the research seemed to center on the early prospectors and miners of the area, including sections along the Snake River where small traces of gold had been found.

Paige had said she had come to Jackson Hole to do an article on the area, so it wasn't a surprise to Jake to find that another division of the folder held copies of email correspondences with an editor, a Susan Shaw from New York. Hoping to find some clue as to where Paige might be, he skimmed through them. Most of the early emails were just brief descriptions of her arrival in town, accompanied by comments from her editor intended to direct her toward the type of article that would be of most interest to readers. Her editor had suggested finding some type of local story. It seemed reasonable to Jake that this would be more interesting than a basic history report.

As Jake continued through the emails, though, it became clear that Paige felt she had stumbled onto something more. She mentioned the prospecting history specifically and implied she was close to solving an old mystery. In response, her editor had encouraged her to pursue the lead. This explained her recent determination to be involved. Coupled with the conversation she had overheard between Frank and Maddie inside the Cowboy Bar, it was all starting to make sense.

This brought Maddie to mind again. How on earth was she involved with all this? Tucking the folder underneath his arm, he closed the door to Paige's car and headed to the Blue Sky Café. Since Maddie had no idea that he knew anything about her involvement, it would be safe to keep with his usual morning pattern. And Frank, as always, would sit at the end of the counter and pretend he didn't know him. There was no reason to avoid going there for coffee and, after his sleepless night, the idea of a fresh cup was now starting to sound appealing.

True to habit, Frank Thompson was sitting in his usual spot, hunched over his coffee in his usual manner. Jake mustered up whatever acting ability he could manage and approached the counter, smiling and joking as he always did.

Maddie, clearly used to playing the same role, did the same, already pouring his black coffee as she spoke.

Jake paid for his coffee and thanked Maddie, which seemed to take much more of an effort than usual. Cupping one hand around the mug and grabbing a daily paper with the other, he retreated to the far corner booth. Accustomed to liking the privacy of this particular spot, it was especially convenient this morning, as it afforded him an opportunity to look over the paperwork in Paige's folder again. He pulled a few of the papers out and read through them, continuing to glance at the door in hopes of seeing Paige walk in.

As he read, he started to see why she had become more and more interested in the history of prospecting in Jackson Hole. It was true that there hadn't been any large findings recorded. But there were many instances of mining trips along the river where nothing was recorded at all. There were many loose ends, leaving open the possibility that more gold had been discovered than reported. Prospectors had often split into small groups, or even gone off individually for hours at a time. Gathering together later to discuss their findings, or lack thereof, around a campfire, it was very feasible that a greedy man might not share his fortune with others. He could easily have hidden his stash, returning later on his own to retrieve it. This all fit in with the story he had heard so many times as a child.

He sat back and thought this through. Paige, with her twinkling eyes and thick, auburn hair, had somehow fallen into all this. He again found himself worrying for her safety and watching the door of the cafe.

Focused on reading, he jumped a little when Maddie approached his table to refill his coffee. He shuffled the papers casually, attempting to appear disinterested in them. It was not until he thanked Maddie for the refill and watched her walk away that it occurred to him that it was out of character for her to bring out a refill. As was typical in a trendy coffee house, drinks and food were served from the counter. Feeling uneasy from this change in pattern, he sipped a little of his coffee refill, pretended to skim the local paper and then headed out the door, waving what he hoped came across as a casual goodbye.

Carrying Paige's folder, he was already thinking through the apology he would have to give for removing it from her car. He could always return the folder and say nothing, but Paige's research could be helpful. He needed to read through her papers more thoroughly. An apology would have to do. Keeping the folder, he made his way back to the truck. He drove home to the ranch house, built a fire and sat quietly, reading and waiting.

CHAPTER TWENTY-ONE

Paige slept soundly for a few hours, exhausted from following Cyrus the evening before. But she was awake early, when the sun was not even yet hinting to rise. She stretched quickly, put her hat back on, tucked her hair up underneath it again and left the barn, peering up and down the road first to be sure the street was deserted. Still dark enough to walk through town unnoticed, she retraced the route she had taken across town with Chester the night before, continuing east until she came to mountain's edge.

She turned north, summoning the will power to ignore the aching muscles she felt from the climb the night before. It was going to be a long hike, especially without the luxury of a horse, but she was determined to retrace her steps. She knew she had to get a closer look at the location Cyrus had reached. She needed to see it in the daylight.

It was hours before she reached the steep grade of the final stretch they had covered the night before. By now, the sun had risen to a mid-morning position and the landscape looked different in the light of day. To her left, the valley stretched out before her with elk grazing and eagles soaring overhead. The Grand Tetons towered beyond that, breathtaking as always in their abrupt rise from the valley floor. Some things do stand the test of time, Paige mused.

Trees hid the terrain in front of her and sharp cliffs of rock rose to her right. She continued on, searching in front of her for the cluster of trees and the boulder that she remembered as their stopping place. Lodgepole pines filled most of the mountainside to her right, while aspens were scattered on the lower levels to her left. But the trio formation she remembered from her trip with Chester was nowhere to be found.

She continued to move forward, taking one cautious step at a time, holding onto small boulders and sturdy tree branches to steady herself as the climb became increasingly severe. Finally she spotted a large boulder ahead, with several trees to the right. It was not until she reached it that she was certain that this was the right spot.

She leaned against the tree closest to the boulder and looked across at the two closest trees. The distances were right, each located in the same place she remembered from the night before. There were other trees behind them, but they were far enough away to not have been visible in the dark of night. This was the right place. Now she just had to locate the spot where Cyrus had stopped, which she knew would be more difficult.

Resting against the tree, she gazed up the mountainside, attempting to estimate the distance between the spot where she now stood and the location where the glow of the lantern had stopped. It had been far enough away to become dim, but still close enough to be seen, which meant that she could see Cyrus's destination from where she stood. And now she had the benefit of daylight. With this in mind, she continued on, proceeding with cautious steps as the rocky trail became increasingly uneven. Taking switchbacks along rock ledges in order to climb higher, she tried not to look down, as the sharp drop only served to make her dizzy. She glanced back occasionally in order to gauge the distance she had traveled beyond the trio of trees. Drawing on memory from the night before, she could estimate the lantern's distance. Reaching a small plateau, she sat down to catch her breath.

She was overwhelmed by the breathtaking view. The town of Jackson was no longer visible, but across from where she sat the Tetons soared into the sky, bathed in morning light. Patches of fog lay across the valley floor. In the foreground the town of Kelly rested alongside the Gros Ventre River, diminutive from the high vantage point. Paige took a deep breath of clean mountain air and then glanced around to appraise the area immediately surrounding her.

It was a narrow ledge, but long, curving around a slight bend to her right. Above her the rocks seemed to rise straight into the sky. There was no way that Cyrus would have been able to climb higher. He would have needed advanced climbing equipment to scale the sheer rock section above the ledge. Tentatively she stood and began to explore the side of the cliff with her hands. The rock was solid with clumps of course brush protruding from occasional splits in the surface. Some of the crevices were only slight indentations, while others appeared to stretch deeper into the rocks.

As Paige rounded a narrow portion of the north end of the ledge a crevice appeared that was noticeably wider than the others. She approached it and peered inside, estimating that the interior stretched back into the cliff a good ten to twelve feet. The overall width was more difficult to determine, as the side walls were not straight. She sized up the opening and determined that, although narrow, it was just wide enough that she could fit through. Not any crazier about dark, confined spaces than she was about heights, she summoned up her courage and slipped inside.

Cool air struck her face almost immediately as she slid into the rock and away from the light. She paused to let her eyes adjust to the darkness and then slowly looked around. The width of the interior was much wider than the opening itself. This wasn't just a wide crevice; it was a cave.

She moved around the interior, estimating its size by running her hands along the inside of the walls. One wall extended a little farther to the side than the other, just enough to form a slight, side indentation. She estimated the large, rear portion of the cavernous space to be about five feet by eight.

As her eyes continued to adjust to the low light, she could see the cave's walls more clearly. Looking back at the entrance and imagining the darkness at night, she guessed that Cyrus had placed his lantern in that location, which would have illuminated the cave while still allowing the dim view of the light they had seen from below.

Paige continued to feel her way around, searching for traces of any area that might serve as a hiding place. Above her the rocky ceiling was solid and unbroken. It wasn't realistic that anything could be hidden that high, gravity itself being one reasonable factor. Running her hands around the middle portions of the wall, she found no trace of any opening. The ground itself seemed firm, as well. It was as she inspected the intersection of the walls and the floor of the cave that she found a pile of small rocks stacked haphazardly against the wall. There was nothing unusual about them, as other similar rocks were scattered around the rest of the floor. Had Paige not been searching for anything in particular, it's not likely she would have noticed them.

Leaning down, she moved the rocks aside, finding only more behind them, these a little bigger than the first group. As she moved them away from the wall, she saw that several were wedged into the wall itself. Loose dirt rested in cracks between the rocks, which were carefully placed to form a layer that matched the flat surface of the wall itself. Grasping the rocks firmly one by one, she pulled them out and set them aside. Eventually a small cavity began to appear.

As she started to reach into the dark space, she was suddenly startled by a rustling noise at the cave's entrance. Her heart rising into her throat, she quickly pressed herself against the side wall, just out of sight of the opening of the cave. A dark, shadow was thrown against the back wall, cast by the sunlight beyond the ledge. Her heart pounding fiercely inside her chest, she closed her eyes tightly and held her breath. Finally, hearing no sound, she opened them slowly and looked around.

The shadow was still there, motionless and silent. She contemplated the shape of its outline, tall and round, thinning out quickly at the bottom. It narrowed at the top, though it was not quite as slender as below. She remained frozen until suddenly the width of the shadow expanded, accompanied by a flapping sound from the front of the cave. Her panic suddenly easing, she peered around the corner to see the silhouette of a large crow standing in the shade of the cave's entrance. Aggravated and breathless from the scare, she quickly shooed the bird away and resumed her search.

It took digging through several additional layers of rocks, each stacked in front of the next, to reach the open space behind it. When she finally did, Paige sat back in nervous anticipation. All of her efforts could have been for nothing. It was possible that there simply was nothing to be found, that she was a victim of an overactive imagination. Cyrus might have hidden it somewhere else. Or there might not have been anything to hide to begin with. Still, she had come this far. It only made sense to follow through.

Tentatively, she crouched down, reaching slowly into the small opening. Patting the surface of the compartment, she felt nothing, other than the foolishness of having gone to such extremes to follow what could easily have been a false hunch. A second search led to the same empty-handed result, as did several additional tries. In one last attempt before giving up, she flattened herself on the cave's floor and inched her way up to the wall. Dust filled her nostrils and gravel scratched across her face as she pressed her shoulder so tightly against the opening that she feared it would become stuck. With her arm stretched as far back as possible, the tips of her fingers finally brushed against the texture of coarse cloth. She attempted to pull the cloth forward, but a substantial weight fought back against her efforts.

Determined, she grasped repeatedly at the cloth with her fingers, finally inching it close enough to grab solidly with her hand. Pulling her body slowly away from the wall, she was able to dislodge the cloth and pull it forward, dragging a bulky object just behind it. Though it didn't feel wide, the entirety of the object was heavy and cumbersome. She fought to pull it toward the small entrance, finding it impossible to bring forward more than an inch at a time. At one point it became lodged just inside the cavity entrance, but after some maneuvering, she was finally able to pull it out and drag it into the light just inside the cave's opening.

Paige sat silent and still for what felt like a long time, though by this point the entire concept of time had ceased to feel reliable. She regarded the sack objectively, figuring it measured a good foot wide, more than a foot long and only a slightly shorter distance in height. Finally gathering her courage, she pulled the cloth sack open, dumping its contents on the dusty floor of the cave.

The sunlight had grown more intense as it had continued to rise in the sky while Paige was inside the cave. It now cast a brilliant glow across the large chunks of golden rock and surrounding flakes of gold dust. There were dozens of nuggets, some measuring three or four inches in diameter. Even in the darkness of the cave, they glittered in the rays of light that filtered through the entrance. Paige sat quietly, listening only to the silence and staring with disbelief at the gold. Moving the sack of gold dust and nuggets to the back of the cave, she returned to the entrance, where she stepped out and leaned back against the cliff wall, looking out across the valley.

She had been right. This alone seemed amazing to her. But being right also posed a problem. Now that she'd found the gold, she had to figure out what to do with it. Moving it to another spot might protect it from being moved again by Cyrus, but there was no reason to think he would move it now. Though his intentions had originally been to share the hiding place with Jeremiah, she knew that, in later years, Jeremiah would pass down the legend of the gold without enough information about its location.

She could take it, but take it where? Provided she was able to find the skeleton key again – she dared not entertain the idea that she wouldn't – how did she know the gold would stay with her as she crossed whatever threshold it was that had brought her to where she was now? Though it seemed incredulous to leave it where it was, now that she had found it, it seemed wrong to alter what she knew to be the future. The only thing to do was to replace the gold where she had found it.

She moved back inside the cave and sat next to the golden rocks, lifting each one up with care and placing it back in the sack. When the treasure was safely tucked inside the cloth, she tied the sack shut and once again stretched out on the floor of the cave, pushing it as far back into the compartment as it would go. She then painstakingly replaced each rock, building layer after layer of wall, until the chamber was identical to the way she had found it.

Climbing down from the ledge slowly, she held tightly to the jagged rocks sticking out along the way. Reaching the trail below, she paused to rest before starting down the mountainside, both fatigued from the physical test of her endurance and feeling dazed from her discovery. But thinking ahead to everything she needed to do, she pushed herself to start heading back to Jackson, a trip which would take a good two hours.

She arrived back in town by mid-afternoon and headed straight to the livery barn. With the sun still high in the sky, rays of light flowed through the barn's rafters and landed directly on the hay covered ground. One wagon was gone, which Paige knew was a sign that Chester was out giving local townsfolk a ride. The barn, however, was not empty. Across the sunlit interior, Paige saw Jeremiah working in one of the stalls, hay flying over his head each time he pushed a pitchfork forward and then pulled it up and back. Paige approached slowly, unsure what she would say when she caught his attention. Several minutes passed as she watched his strong, lean back at work before he became aware of her presence and turned around.

"Can I help you with something?" Jeremiah said, his eyes squinting slightly to see who the visitor was.

"I just…I just…" Paige started to speak, but then found herself at a loss for words. What would she say, anyway? That she just wanted to see him? That she knew where the gold was that Cyrus had hidden from him? That someday he would have a wonderful great-grandson who would be able to carry out the legend that he would pass down to his son, who would in turn pass it on? None of this would make any sense.

Hearing the soft voice that came from what appeared to be a young man, Jeremiah put the pitchfork down and took a few steps closer. He saw that the person who had spoken was wearing dirt-covered overalls and that the accompanying hat was equally scuffed and covered with dust. The face below the brim of the hat, however, was soft and delicate. A few smudges of dirt stretched across the person's forehead and the eyes appeared dazed. Stepping forward, he reached gently for the hat and slowly pulled it off.

Paige's hair fell in waves around her shoulders as Jeremiah's eyes widened in surprise.

"I know you," he said slowly, stepping backwards a couple feet to take in Paige's attire. "I saw you at the saloon, though you certainly looked..." Jeremiah paused, choosing his words carefully, "a little different then." He began to relax from the initial shock of seeing the clearly feminine hair cascade down. A gentle smile crossed his face.

"Yes," Paige said cautiously. 'I've been out hiking this morning," she added, not sure what other explanation she could give.

"Ah," Jeremiah responded, as if this made sense. "Well I guess you certainly couldn't do that in the elegant dress you had on before," he said.

"No, I don't think so," Paige agreed. She looked at Jeremiah, noticing how strong his features were, how rich the brown of his hair was and how attractive she found his eyes. As she had come to suspect, all these things looked familiar. She had seen the same face in Jake. The resemblance was almost astonishing.

"I guess I'm a little scuffed up myself," Jeremiah admitted, noticing the attention his appearance was getting. He looked down at his hay-covered clothing and brushed a few strands to the floor.

"Oh, I'm sorry," Paige apologized quickly, realizing she had been staring longer than would normally be polite. "I didn't mean to be rude, it's just...well, you know, you remind me of someone I know." She wished she could tell Jeremiah what she saw when she looked at him, but knew it wasn't possible.

"Anyway, I just came by to..." her voice trailed off, unable to find a way to finish the statement. She just came by to what? Just to make sure she understood how the pieces of the past and future fit together? None of it would make sense to him. She wasn't even sure it made sense to her. Finding no suitable explanation to give him, she glanced around the barn, anxiously seeking a way to change the subject.

"What are these?" Paige asked quickly, stepping over to a post studded with iron hooks. She reached out and gathered several hanging straps of leather into her hand.

Jeremiah followed her to the barn post and leaned against it with one arm, clearly amused.

"Now, I think you're just joking around with me, ma'am," he said, not even trying to hide his amusement.

"Really," Paige pushed on, avoiding his eyes while inspecting the riding gear closely. "I didn't ride in New...I mean, I didn't do much riding in Denver."

"Chester was surely right about you," Jeremiah said, running the back of his hand across his forehead. "You're an odd one, you are." He paused briefly before adding, "But a pretty one, I have to admit."

"Thank you," Paige said, blushing. "Though I suspect you mean pretty odd, not odd and pretty," she added, laughing.

"Well, that too," Jeremiah quipped with mock seriousness, before shaking his head and smiling as he turned away.

Taking slow, ambling steps, he moved across the barn to the back door, putting his hands on his hips and peering up at the sky. He walked with the same shy, yet self-confident manner that characterized Jake's movements. Paige felt a smile creep across her face, which she attempted unsuccessfully to hide as Jeremiah turned around and walked back over, reaching over her shoulder for one of the halters on the post. He moved close enough for her to catch the smell of his skin, to feel his breath fall softly on her cheek. It seemed he lingered for a few seconds before stepping away and speaking up.

"I imagine you'd probably like a sip of cool water if you've been running all over the mountains," he said politely. Paige didn't miss seeing the twinkle in his eye.

"That does sound tempting," she replied, realizing that she did feel thirsty after the morning's trek up the rocky cliff and back.

"There's a covered bucket of water out back, in the shed just past that small wagon. Help yourself," Jeremiah said. "I've got these stalls to finish and then these horses need saddling up, but the key's hanging on the wall over there." He motioned toward the back door of the barn with his hand as he picked up the pitchfork and leaned against it.

She walked toward the back door of the barn, certain she could feel Jeremiah's eyes following her. It seemed odd that he hadn't offered to bring the water to her. But by the time she reached the door, she already suspected what she would find. Hanging on a rusty nail, a ray of sunlight hitting it in a striking contrast to the barn's dark, wooden walls, was the skeleton key.

She started to reach forward and then hesitated, turning around. Jeremiah still stood there, leaning against the pitchfork and watching her. He was silent, a gentle smile on his face. Paige slowly returned the smile, finding the will to whisper across the space between them.

"Thank you, Jeremiah," she said softly before turning back towards the wall. Without pausing this time, she reached for the key.

CHAPTER TWENTY-TWO

The sudden pounding on the front door startled Jake and caused him to jump. His nerves were already frayed from a long night spent watching the fire and waiting anxiously for any sign of Paige. He stood up quickly and turned away from the fireplace. But he barely had time to take a step forward before the front door flew open and Paige burst in. She looked exhausted and somewhat disheveled, but her face was flushed with excitement and her eyes were wide and animated.

"I know where it's buried," Paige exclaimed. She leaned against the wing-backed chair, taking in quick gulps of air, attempting to catch her breath.

"How..." Jake started to ask, but Paige immediately shook her head and brushed the question away.

"Jake, there's no way I can explain this, not any way that would be believable," Paige said in a rush of words. "But I'm telling you, I know where it is. You've got to trust me on this."

There was no use arguing. Jake moved the logs in the fire around, so that only embers remained, then doused them with water to make sure they were out. He then grabbed his keys and headed for his truck, with Paige already a good twenty feet ahead.

Jake drove carefully, but couldn't help pushing a little heavily on the accelerator at times. At Paige's direction, he headed towards the main highway. As he approached the Gros Ventre junction, he signaled to turn right, but Paige indicated that he needed to turn left, instead.

"Just head toward town," Paige said anxiously.

"But I'm sure..." Jake started to argue, keeping his foot pressed down on the brake pedal.

"No," Paige said, cutting him off quickly. "You've been looking in the wrong place. Turn left. I'll show you where we need to go."

Paige kept her eyes to the north as they headed south along the highway. She surveyed the flat, open land that stretched across to the mountains on the east side of the valley. A few elk grazed in the field, midway between the road and the foothills. As they approached the town, Paige watched the landscape carefully, noting where slabs of rock began rising abruptly and judging the distance between those points and the town.

"That's where it is," she said suddenly, pointing across the field at a snow-capped area at the top of the mountains. "That's the right distance from town. I'm sure that's the place."

Jake turned his head to follow Paige's outstretched arm.

"Sleeping Indian?" he responded, looking at the mountains and then back at Paige.

"What's Sleeping Indian?" Paige asked.

"Look up at the top of the mountain," Jake said. "If you look carefully, you'll see the Indian's face and headdress to the right and the body across to the left."

Paige studied the curves of the mountain top until the image Jake was describing registered.

"You're right," she said slowly, "I just hadn't noticed it before. That makes sense, then..." Her voice trailed off as she thought about the phrases she had overheard in Tuttle's Saloon.

"What makes sense?" Jake asked, more and more confused by Paige's statements.

"Nothing," Paige answered quickly. "In fact, I'm not sure anything makes sense anymore. I've had to put a lot of things together. Anyway, we're going to have to hike in there from town. We'll follow the edge of the mountainside."

Jake gave her another puzzled look. "We don't have to hike in from town. I mean, we'll have to hike up the mountain section, but there's a road that leads up there, back behind the Elk Refuge."

"There is?" Paige asked, surprised.

Jake laughed. "You know, for someone so sure of where we're going, you sure don't know how we're getting there."

Paige motioned impatiently for Jake to keep driving as she drew upon memory and threw directions out along the way. Once in town, they took a left at Broadway and traveled east, taking another left to head down the dirt road behind the National Elk Refuge. First smooth and flat, it grew increasingly rough as they drove on.

"It's a good thing we brought your truck," Paige said, thankful for the distance they'd be able to cover without having to hike, or go on horseback, for that matter.

As the road continued, it became narrow and uneven. The recent rain had left scattered potholes and muddy puddles along the route. Rolling the window down, Paige glanced ahead at the winding turns before them. They still had a good distance to go. The truck followed the road as far as possible, veering to the right at several forks and finally approaching a steep, wooded area, where they pulled over and parked.

"This is as far as we can take the truck," Jake said, turning off the engine. 'But there's a footpath up ahead somewhere on the right."

Paige climbed out of the truck and headed immediately for the mountainside. Jake grabbed a jacket and backpack from the rear of the truck, hustling to catch up. The untended trail was not difficult to locate. As the incline of the slope increased, the foliage grew thicker. Though the trees were taller and more numerous in some areas, much of the landscape was as she remembered. It was some time before they came to the trio of trees and large boulder, but when they did, there was no question in Paige's mind that it was the right place.

"They're so tall now…" Paige muttered absentmindedly, standing in the middle of the three trees and looking up, her neck stretched back.

"You know, Paige, you're really acting a little strange," Jake said hesitantly. "Maybe this isn't the best time to try this."

"We're not stopping now," Paige said firmly, turning towards the upward slope and stepping forward. Jake shook his head, resigning himself to continuing up the trail. Even if she had no idea what she was doing, she was clearly determined. He'd follow along, if only to make sure she made it up and back safely.

For what seemed like a long time, they fought the rough terrain, climbing over fallen trees and rocky stretches, losing and catching their footing several times. At one point Paige slipped, sliding a good two feet off the side of the trail. Standing back up, she brushed the dirt off and moved forward, ignoring another offer from Jake to turn back.

Paige felt confident she was proceeding forward on track, but as they reached the ledge she became disoriented. The view to the valley matched what she remembered, but the ledge itself barely resembled the one she had stood on before. Not nearly as wide, it was covered with piles of fallen rocks, leaving little flat area on which to stand. The surface was covered with thick brush and the edge seemed to drop off more sharply than before. It was also much shorter, ending in a massive stack of rock and brush only a few feet from where they stood.

"This has to keep going," Paige said, pointing in the direction of the tall stack of rocks. She walked over to the pile and attempted to look over the top. Taking a step up, her foot just slid back down, bringing a few rocks tumbling down.

"Paige, this is too dangerous," Jake said, looking over the ledge at the sharp drop. "Those rocks are not secure. It's too risky to continue." He paused before adding, "And we're not even sure there's anything here."

Paige turned sharply to face Jake. Before she even spoke, he knew his arguments weren't going to convince her to turn back.

"This is where it is, Jake! This is what you've been looking for all these years! How can you turn away from it now?"

Paige pivoted around to face the rocks again and began brushing some away, leaving only the largest, sturdiest ones in place. Eventually, a clearing opened up and she climbed forward, where she looked over the remaining pile of rocks to find a narrow section of the ledge that continued on. Jake steadied her as she crossed over the rock pile and dropped down on the other side. He was just seconds behind her.

The ledge grew increasingly narrow, its edge dropping off sharply and showing signs of heavy erosion. Turning sideways to continue, Paige and Jake inched their way along the rock wall, feeling relief when they reached a wider section just before it ended abruptly. Paige turned to face the steep rock wall, searching the surface for any cracks or crevices.

"What is it?" Jake asked, watching her confused expression.

"I don't understand," Paige said. "There should be a cave here, but there's nothing." She continued to inspect the area, but found no trace of any opening. Discouraged, she sat down against the wall and looked out over the valley. It seemed impossible that she could remember the way here and yet be wrong about the end of the trail.

Deep in thought, she didn't hear Jake start to speak, but as the sound of his voice registered, she turned towards him.

"What did you say?" she asked quickly, "Just a minute ago?"

"Earthquakes," Jake repeated. "There've been plenty of earthquakes in this area over the years. I don't know where you got the idea there was a cave here, but if it's something you found in your research of the area's history, it may have gotten covered by shifting rocks during earthquake activity."

"That could explain changes in the cliff," Paige thought out loud, looking around her. With a sinking feeling, she realized the cave might not exist at all anymore. There would be no way to reach the gold if nothing but solid rock surrounded it now.

She stood quickly and turned toward the rocky surface, kneeling down to inspect the area where the cliff met the ledge. Brushing aside dirt with her hands, she began digging faster. Jake, following her lead, started digging a few feet away.

The ground was packed solidly against the rock, but slowly began to break off into small clods of dirt. Using loose rocks as picks, Paige and Jake smashed the sharp edges against the wall, breaking off more of the dirt and releasing larger rocks from the packed terrain. Hours passed and the muscles in their arms ached from repetitive use. Yet only small sections of the wall fell forward.

"It's no use, Paige," Jake said, setting the sharp rock he'd been using down on the ledge and urging her to do the same.

Paige, exhausted and discouraged, didn't respond, though she was starting to fear that Jake might be right.

She lifted her arm high yet again and let the rock crash sharply against the wall with full force. One last time she repeated the motion, at which point the rocky surface suddenly budged inward, rather than tumbling forward onto the ledge like before. Paige stared at the wall and then shouted over her shoulder to Jake.

"It's here!" she yelled, repeatedly striking the area that had given in. With a few more blows, the dirt against the rock also crumbled inward, leaving a small hole in its place. Jake moved over by Paige and wedged the rock he was holding into the hole. With a little force, additional rock also dislodged and fell inward. One section at a time, they worked furiously together as more pieces of the wall fell away, leaving a growing opening into a dark space within the rocky cliff. Finally, they determined the opening was wide enough for them to fit through, one at a time.

With Jake adamant about leading, Paige followed behind until they were both crouched down inside the darkness. As opposed to the changes on the outside, the interior of the cave looked much the same. Heading quickly to the back of the cave and then into the side extension, Paige located the small inner cavern, kicked a clutter of rocks out of the way and threw herself flat against the ground. Sliding her arm into the opening and easing her body up against the wall, she reached in as far as she could, but felt nothing with her fingers. Trying to push herself closer to the wall, she stretched until it seemed her shoulder would pop out of its socket. Still she felt nothing. Even the back wall was out of reach.

"My arm's not long enough," Paige said. "You're going to have to do this." She backed away from the wall, sitting up and moving aside to allow Jake room to approach the opening.

Sliding down on the floor, Jake repeated the same motions Paige had made, pushing his shoulder up against the wall and feeling the interior of the cavern with his hand.

"Do you feel the back wall?" Paige asked anxiously.

Jake grunted a little as he moved around on the ground. "I feel the back wall with my fingers, but there's nothing there."

"Keep trying," Paige urged. "Search the sides."

"Nothing," Jake said, stopping for a minute to catch his breath.

"Try again," Paige insisted, closing her eyes and praying they hadn't gone to such extreme effort in vain. She watched as Jake resumed the stretch with his arm, feeling around for another thirty seconds or so until he let out a sharp gasp.

"I've got something," he shouted, pushing his body even flatter against the wall and struggling to dislodge the rough item his fingers had grasped. It took numerous attempts before he finally eased away from the wall, pulling a dusty sack out, clods of embedded dirt falling away from it as he dragged it to the middle of the cave's floor.

Together they stared at the crusty object in silence, Paige out of gratitude that she had not been mistaken in dragging

Jake up the cliff and Jake out of sheer disbelief. Finally Paige looked up and spoke.

"You open it, Jake," she said quietly. "It's yours. You should be the one to open it."

Jake glanced up at Paige briefly, a look of nervous anticipation in his eyes.

Slowly, he reached for the sack and tugged on the lumpy knot tying it closed. Decay on the rope's fibers made it impossible to untie them, so he pulled out a Swiss army knife from his pocket and sliced his way through the stubborn strands until they fell away. Pausing only to take a deep breath, he held the sack up at an angle and let the contents spill out on the cave's floor.

There was only the slightest light flowing in through the small opening of the cave, but it was enough to see the sparkle of the nuggets that fell on the ground. Jake stared at the pile of gold, unable to speak. Paige watched him silently, wondering what it must feel like for him to reach the goal he had dreamed of most of his life.

"Now what," Jake finally said, sounding lost in the echo of the cave.

"That's up to you, Jake," Paige said quietly. "This is your family's legend and history. Only you can decide what to do with it." Leaving Jake to think, she returned to the cave's entrance and climbed through the opening. She brushed aside some of the rocks they had dislodged earlier and sat down on the ledge, looking out over the valley.

Jake remained in the cave for some time and then emerged to sit beside Paige.

"Look at this valley," Jake sighed. "It's a treasure in itself, gold or no gold."

"I can't disagree," Paige responded, looking across the rolling buttes and over to the Tetons before bringing her eyes to the closer section of valley below.

"That's Kelly, isn't it?" Paige asked, looking at the small buildings from above. "And the Gros Ventre River, running next to it?"

"You're getting to know the area," Jake said in agreement, reaching out with his arm to point towards the town. "Just think, Great-Grandpa Norris and his back-stabbing partner both lived within view of this mountain."

"And now so do you," Paige added.

Jake nodded his head. "You know, I bought that old ranch because it would put me in the same area they lived in, thinking that would help me find the gold. But all this time, I was looking in the wrong direction, west to the Tetons."

Jake leaned back on his arms and sighed. In all the time he had invested, searching for the gold, he'd never once considered the east side of the valley.

"You know, that area was called the 'Bridge' by settlers back in the early 1900's," Paige pointed out, remembering information she'd found through the National Park Service.

"Really," Jake responded, clearly surprised.

"Yes, really," Paige answered. "Early homesteaders built a timber bridge across the river. There was quite a town there before that flood wiped it out. Mercantile, hotel, dance hall, sawmill, feed supply and livery barn, etc."

"So, then..." Jake said, tumbling images around in his head, "those marks at the bottom of Frank's map... the ones I thought might be a ladder..."

"...were a bridge," Paige finished the sentence for him.

"And the round smudge that I thought covered something else..." Jake continued.

"...was a cave," Paige filled in again.

Silence settled in, replacing conversation. Paige felt exhaustion creeping into her bones and Jake's thoughts tumbled wildly within the realization that the long-awaited dream had become reality. Finally Jake spoke up.

"We have to leave it," he said quietly, so quietly that Paige was almost sure she had misunderstood him.

Seeing the stunned expression on Paige's face, he spoke up again, this time loud enough that there was no question what he was saying.

"I can't take it, Paige," Jake said. "This is the legend that has been passed down to me through my great-grandfather, my grandfather and my father. It's meant to be passed down again. I have to leave it."

Paige sat still, trying to take in Jake's words and reasoning. It seemed crazy to have gone to such lengths to find the gold he had dreamed about his whole life, only to leave it behind. But it was the legend that had kept him going, not the gold itself. Maybe it was the legend that would keep others going in the future. As crazy as it seemed, she could half-way understand his twisted reasoning. Besides, it wasn't her decision to make.

Jake climbed back into the cave, while Paige remained outside, her back resting against the cliff wall. This was something he needed to do on his own.

She looked across the valley at the Grand Tetons, feeling the strong sense of area history and the relativity of time as she had come to know it. She compared her own journey to the history Jackson Hole's towering peaks had seen long before. It all amounted to a split second, the passage of time. Even the century of change she had witnessed was nothing compared to the open expanse of the future.

Jake returned to the ledge and Paige stood to help him. Slowly, they worked to rebuild the surface of the cliff, stuffing dirt and twigs between rocks to hold them firmly in place. Layer upon layer, they built multiple barriers to separate the cave from the outer ledge. Gathering dirt clods and brush, they scattered these against the outside section that hid the cave's entrance until the surface blended with the rock wall itself.

Moving back along the ledge, they reached the tall rock pile that they had broken down before, crossed to the other side and built that up, as well. With the surrounding rocks and brush stacked high, the ledge behind was well hidden.

Carefully, they retraced their steps down the mountainside, finally reaching Jake's truck and heading back to town in silence.

CHAPTER TWENTY-THREE

Paige stepped through the front door of The Blue Sky Café and took her place in line. The wait had grown shorter, even in just the few days that she and Jake had avoided the place. The tourist season continued to slip further into the past.

She eyed the baked goods with approval. All her favorites were there: raspberry-orange muffins, maple-pecan scones and zucchini-cinnamon bread. The chalkboard announced lunch specials for the day: Roasted Tomato-Basil Soup, Greek Salad with Kalamata Olives and Feta Cheese and a Grilled Chicken Panini, served with sliced avocado and fresh cantaloupe.

"Well, look who's here," Maddie said - a little too cheerfully, it seemed - as Paige approached the counter. "I thought you must've gone back to New York. Haven't seen you in here the last few days." Turning away briefly, Maddie waved to a local who was heading out the door after adding cream and sugar to his coffee.

Not crediting herself with the same acting ability as Maddie obviously had, Paige kept things simple.

"You're pretty much right on both counts," Paige said lightly. "I'm headed back to New York in just a few days. And I haven't been in because I had to finish up an article and get it sent back there by today." Paige pointed to one of the raspberry-orange muffins in the case, which Maddie grabbed with a square of wax paper.

"Coffee? Latte?" Maddie offered, holding up an empty mug as a question mark.

"Why not," Paige said, slipping into the conspicuously empty counter seat where Old Man Thompson usually sat. "Coffee will be fine."

"So how did that go?" Maddie asked lightly. "Your article, I mean."

Paige shook her head and let out what she hoped sounded like a sufficiently discouraged sigh.

"Not as well as I hoped it would," Paige said as she reached for the coffee mug. "I thought I was onto something really interesting, but it turned out to be a false lead." She blew a puff of air across the top of the mug to cool the surface of the coffee. Without looking up, she knew she had Maddie's full attention.

"What I mean is," Paige continued casually, "Jackson Hole is such an amazing area. There're all sorts of things to write about - outdoor activities, the tourism industry, the wildlife and conservation efforts, etc. But I was convinced I'd stumbled into a whole realm of hidden history. It would have made for an outstanding exclusive, the sort of thing that could really help my career."

"And instead?" Maddie prodded, wiping down a countertop near Paige's seat.

"Instead, I just ended up with a basic article about the area." Paige repeated her earlier sigh for good measure. "Don't get me wrong," she added quickly, feigning an apologetic tone. "You have a beautiful valley here and a rich history. Our readers will be interested. It's just personally..." She let her voice trail off. "Well, I guess I was just hoping there was more. I thought..."

"You thought...?" Maddie pushed her for more information, exactly as Paige hoped she would.

Paige set her coffee mug down and leaned forward, lowering her voice to a whisper.

"OK, I know this will sound crazy, but I thought..." she paused and glanced around, as if checking to make sure the café was empty, before turning back to Maddie. "I thought I had found out about some gold that was hidden in the hills a long time ago."

"Well!" Maddie exclaimed, causing Paige to jump, in spite of having anticipated the reaction. "Well," Maddie repeated more calmly, obviously pulling herself together. "That would have made quite a good story, I'm sure."

Paige shook her head, appearing exasperated with herself.

"It sure would have. Imagine if I'd pulled a story like that together." Paige was actually starting to feel self-pity, she sounded so convincing. She wisely stifled a sudden impulse to laugh.

Maddie walked around the end of the counter and picked up two empty mugs that customers had left on a table. Setting them in a bus tray, she casually asked, "What even gave you the idea of this crazy story? It sounds pretty far-fetched." Paige had to admit she admired Maddie's determination to pry more information out of her.

"Sheesh, this will sound even more clueless on my part, but I kind of got swept up in this by a guy I met here."

"Really!" Maddie rolled her eyes in girl-to-girl sympathy.

"Yes, really," Paige confessed. "And it turns out the guy was just gullible, believing some story he'd heard from his uncle...no, wait, maybe his grandfather. I don't know - someone in his family. Anyway, even he realizes now it was just some sort of tall tale."

Paige stood up, fumbled around in her purse and pulled out several dollars, causing crumpled receipts, lip gloss and numerous other items to fall out of the over-stuffed handbag.

"Always the same problem," Paige laughed as she bent over to retrieve the wayward contents. "I never seem to learn that a purse can't hold a suitcase worth of stuff."

"You're not the only one," Maddie agreed. "Doesn't matter what size the purse is, either. It's never big enough for everything."

"Isn't that the truth," Paige replied lightly. She gathered up her belongings quickly, tossed the purse strap over her shoulder and left the money next to her empty mug. Dropping the untouched muffin in a small bag, she shrugged her shoulders as a final statement.

"Let me guess," Maddie inquired with a grin. "The guy was good-looking?"

Paige didn't have to pretend to blush, it came so easily.

"You've got it," she admitted. "Now who's the gullible one?"

"Hey, honey, it happens to the best of us," Maddie called out as Paige waved from the doorway.

* * * *

To: Susan Shaw
From: Paige MacKenzie

Re: Jackson Hole Article

Hi Susan,
I'm attaching a final draft of the article on Jackson Hole. As you'll see, it turned out that the buried treasure theory was a

false lead, though I know it would've made a great story. On the other hand, I was able to gather an exceptional amount of research on the area's history. Both the local library and the Jackson Hole Historical Society were helpful. Conversations with long-time residents of the area added a lot of perspective, as well - things I wouldn't have found in history books.

I'll be packing up and heading back to New York shortly. I just want to take a few more days to enjoy the area. It's truly amazing. You'll have to make a point of seeing it sometime.

See you soon,

Paige

*   *   *

To: Paige MacKenzie
From: Susan Shaw

Re: Jackson Hole Article

Hi Paige,

Well, I have to admit I was disappointed to hear that the buried treasure lead was false. I guess that's the stuff of movies, right?

However, I'm very excited about the article you did send. The historical aspects are so real, so convincing! I was practically sneezing from the dust while reading about Jackson in the early 1900's! Several staff members here have read it and all say the same thing. I don't know how you did it, but you are clearly a genius at research.

Love the photos of current times, too – the old barns, cabins, buck-rail fences, as well as the hectic shots of the town square. Good stuff.

It will be great to see you,

Susan

CHAPTER TWENTY-FOUR

Paige raised her voice to compensate for the hollow clatter of horse hooves against rocks. She was trying her best to keep up with Jake's side of the conversation, but tossing comments back and forth from one saddle to another was difficult.

"What did you say?" she yelled, feeling a little awkward shouting in the direction of a horse's derriere. Jake had insisted on leading the way along the trail, though he was staying as close to Paige's horse as possible.

Jake swiveled his head around and grinned. Paige sensed a tinge of smug satisfaction on his part. He was clearly the more experienced rider.

"I said lean back a little as we head down this hill." Jake motioned ahead at a section of trail they were approaching.

"Shouldn't I lean forward?" Paige questioned. "That's the direction we're going."

"No, ma'am," Jake replied with a slightly exaggerated drawl. "You want to lean forward if you're going uphill and back if you're heading down."

For the most part, Paige was comfortable on the sturdy, medium-sized horse that Jake had picked out for her to ride. The calm, gentle nature of the animal was reassuring and its golden mane blended in with the surrounding fall foliage, the striking yellow and orange leaves of the valley's aspens.

It had been a week since they had found the gold in the cave under Sleeping Indian, enough time to get some rest. And enough time for Paige to complete her article. Jake had started in on projects around the ranch to bide his time while Paige took several days to finish up her work. But once she was done, he'd gotten down to the serious business of showing her what Jackson Hole had to offer.

"How're you holding up, cowgirl?" Jake asked as he helped Paige down from her saddle and tied both horses to a tree. They'd stopped at the bottom of the hill, finding a good sitting log alongside the sparkling blue water of Jackson Lake.

"Holding up just fine, thank you," Paige replied, defying the shakiness her legs felt upon hitting the ground.

"Between horseback riding and whitewater rafting on the Snake River, which did you enjoy more?" Jake asked light-heartedly.

"Both," announced Paige, not only to tease him, but because it was true.

"And the tram ride to Rendezvous Peak over at Teton Village?" he added

"That, too," Paige said laughing, "Though you might have warned me we'd be heading up to 10,000 ft. in altitude."

"Better to leave some things to surprise. Besides, it was 10,450." Jake countered with a wink.

A hush settled over the lake and a lull fell into the conversation. Tiny waves rippled at the edge of the water and muffled voices of hikers echoed across from trails and canyons. The entire valley felt quietly alive with the sounds of twigs snapping, distant kayaks paddling and osprey calling out to each other. Paige was amazed how everything came together as a whole: the visual elements, the natural surroundings, the voices of hikers. Even the scents of pine and fresh mountain air blended in with everything else. It all seemed united; it was all intertwined.

Several moments passed in silence while Paige tried to absorb everything around her, as well as all that had happened in the course of a few weeks. Just as she had sensed, when she first arrived in Jackson Hole, her time there had become much more than a work assignment. It had given her a glimpse into her own heart, had given her the space to slow down and just breathe. These weeks had also opened her eyes to a different way of life, one filled with adventure and possibilities, not the least of which was sitting beside her now at the water's edge.

She turned to sneak a glance at Jake, only to find he was already watching her, a slight hint of a smile in his expression. It did not surprise her to find his eyes mirrored her own thoughts. Instinctively, she returned his smile and did not move her eyes away from his as he reached over to brush a wisp of hair off her forehead. And as he leaned forward to kiss her, the only sounds she could hear were those of soft waves lapping at the lake's shore.

CHAPTER TWENTY-FIVE

The lights were dim and a rendition of Patsy Cline's "Crazy" floated down from the bar above as Paige and Jake descended the stairs to the converted basement and slid into a cozy booth in the Million Dollar Cowboy Steakhouse. A small votive candle flickered on the table. White linen napkins stood folded at each place setting, an elegant atmosphere amidst the gnarled wood and western décor.

Paige and Jake had not spoken of the gold during the last few days. It had been a luxury to just enjoy time with each other, without having to focus energy on anything else. They also hadn't talked about the fact that Paige would be leaving soon, yet the anticipation of her departure was constantly present. She had gathered her belongings and packed her car. But she had pushed away thoughts of leaving, in order to enjoy their remaining time together.

Now, the night before her departure, Paige looked across the table at Jake, who skimmed the menu quickly, before setting it down on the table. Looking up at Paige, she was again moved by the depth of his eyes and the warm expression in his face.

"Have anything you want," Jake said smiling, as he nodded towards the menu. "This is a celebration. For all you did to help me and for my being lucky enough to have met you."

"I think I'm the lucky one, Jake." Paige returned his smile. "I never expected this trip to bring me such adventure and so much joy." She glanced at her menu before setting it aside, telling Jake to choose for both of them.

Jake ordered two signature "Cowboy Cut" ribeye steaks, along with a bottle of Dom Perignon. Celebrating a mission well-accomplished, they sipped the fine champagne and talked over details of the recent weeks.

"I had a bit of a run-in with Frank the other day," Jake offered as he held his champagne glass out to meet Paige's in a toast. "He wasn't too pleased to see me. Seems he didn't take too well to my cursing him out for leading me on a wild goose chase."

"A wild goose chase," Paige repeated with a smile. "He really thinks you've given up?" She had to admit it would be the best possible outcome.

"Oh, yeah, I think he's convinced," Jake replied, nodding his head. "I didn't mince words when I told him how much I resented having a good year's worth of my time wasted."

"Sounds like you have a hidden acting streak in you," Page laughed, imagining the heated exchange between the two men.

"Well, yes and no, the way I see it," Jake explained. "It's true that he wasted my time. I never would have found anything with the lousy half-clues he was feeding me."

"You mean the lousy half-clues that Maddie was feeding him," Paige pointed out, "so that he could pass them on to you."

"Excellent point," Jake agreed. "Speaking of clues, I still don't understand how you could have had such a good hunch about where it was hidden."

Paige stretched her neck to one side and then the other. As an excuse to not meet Jake's eyes for a moment, it worked. As a means of stalling to come up with a plausible explanation, it didn't.

"Let's just say I did a little research and then followed my instincts. Sometimes a hunch just turns out to be right," Paige stated casually, hoping Jake would leave it at that.

"That's not much of an explanation," Jake pointed out, though his expression of resignation made it clear he knew it was the best he would get.

"Maybe some day I'll be able to explain it better, Jake," Paige sighed, wondering how she could ever explain something she didn't even understand herself. "For now, that's the best I can do."

Hearty dinner plates arrived, each steak accompanied by a plump Idaho baked potato, steam escaping from under melting butter and chives. Paige laughed at the sight of the meal, knowing she'd barely be able to put a dent in the generous portions.

"So, do you think Maddie and Frank will ever stop searching for the gold?" Jake asked, shooting a quick smile at Paige and reaching for the chilled bottle in an ice bucket beside the table.

Paige laughed and held her glass out to allow Jake to refill it.

"I don't know," she said, "Maddie had a hard time hiding her relief when I stopped by the cafe and told her I'd been wrong about there being any gold buried in Jackson Hole."

"Ah...good move," Jake said, with admiration.

"And then there's the map. I sort of 'accidentally' dropped it in a shuffle of clutter that fell out of my purse, while paying for coffee."

"Another map?" Jake set his champagne glass down and leaned forward out of curiosity.

"Yes, the decoy idea we talked about. This map was similar to the ones Frank passed you, but had additional notes about narrowing down the location of the treasure."

"Which would be..," Jake asked, eyebrows raised.

"Somewhere up Cascade Canyon, of course. Though the notes leave it iffy as to whether it's up in Hurricane Pass or around Lake Solitude and down partway into Paintbrush Canyon. I figure if they decide to give it another shot, that'll keep them busy for awhile." Paige definitely looked quite pleased with herself.

"Nice," Jake smiled with approval as he leaned back in the booth. "You think she bought it?"

Paige nodded while taking a quick sip of champagne, a move that turned out to be hardly graceful, but hit Jake as endearing, nonetheless.

"She definitely bought it," Paige said. "At least the part about my being sure there wasn't any gold. And she could barely keep from smiling when I said I'd be headed back to New York soon."

A quiet pause settled over the table as both Paige and Jake absorbed the spoken words. Finally, Jake broke the silence.

"And what will she think when you come back?" Jake asked, nonchalantly.

This time it was Paige who had trouble keeping from smiling as she leaned back in the booth.

"Just what makes you think I'll come back?" she countered, trying hard to keep a straight face.

"Oh, nothing in particular," Jake replied casually, his expression clearly showing that he wasn't worried.

"Nothing in particular," Paige repeated, watching him closely to see if he really was as confident as he appeared.

"Well, I mean nothing in particular except a comment that Dan McElroy made the other day when I saw him at the hardware store." Jake now took his turn trying to keep a straight face.

Paige sighed and set her glass down while waiting for Jake to toss out what she knew would follow. It wasn't long before he did.

"Yeah...something about...," Jake stretched his response out, if only for the sheer pleasure of watching Paige squirm. "...something about being glad his cabin tenant had decided to extend her rental a few months.

"You brat," Paige said with a tone of mock reprimand, adding quickly, "It's just for business, you know."

"Of course," Jake said quickly.

"To work on another article," Paige added.

"Naturally," Jake quipped in return.

"Actually, I'm serious about that part. I just didn't say anything so it would be a surprise." Paige sent him a smug smile, pleased that she had upstaged his own secret.

"Really," Jake replied, his teasing tone replaced with genuine interest.

"Seriously," Page repeated. "It seems they had to pull a story from publication this week and dropped the Jackson Hole history piece in at the last minute. Susan said the response was so positive that they want to do a series on the Old West."

"Well, what do you know," Jake said, clearly pleased.

"So, of course, I had no choice but to accept the assignment for the series," Paige stated casually. "After all, work is work."

"Of course," Jake quickly agreed.

The conversation paused while their waiter cleared plates from the table and offered a dessert menu for them to look over. Enticed by the tempting choices, they ordered a huckleberry crème brulee to share, along with two espressos, which quickly landed on the table.

"I'll need to stay back east for two weeks or so," Paige said, sipping slowly from the demitasse of strong brew. Setting it down, she followed Jake's lead and dipped a spoon into the sweet dessert.

"Susan will want an outline of proposed western areas to cover," Paige continued. "Places that would have unique backgrounds, that sort of thing. I'm sure there are plenty of possibilities."

"No question about that." Jake agreed, without hesitation. "There's a rich history of mining in many areas out here, not just for gold, but silver, too. And for sapphires up in Montana. Also, there's the development of the railroads. Not to mention tales of outlaws. Oh, and ghost towns, and…"

"OK, I get it," Paige said, laughing and setting down her spoon.

Jake reached across the table and took Paige's hand in his, running his fingers across her soft skin and asking her what she was thinking.

"Well, I was thinking…" Paige started to speak and then hesitated. They hadn't talked specifically about the journey up to Sleeping Indian and the decisions that followed the discovery of the gold.

"I was just wondering," she asked quietly, "what you would have done if you had decided to keep the gold. What I mean is, I think it's amazing, the decision you made. But you must have wondered yourself, since then, what you might have done with it." She waited quietly, hoping her question had not overstepped any lines. This was Jake's business, not her own. But he had asked what she was thinking, so that was what he got.

To her relief, Jake's smile started to widen. He waited for the approaching waiter to clear the dessert plate from the table and then spoke once he had walked away.

"Actually, you're right, I have thought about it. I've thought about it quite a bit," he said, obviously fighting back a laugh. "For example, if I'd kept any of it, I could have..."

Paige watched, puzzled, as he let go of her hand and leaned back. Reaching into his pocket, he slowly pulled out a small object. She threw Jake a look of surprise when she saw a delicate gold chain wrapped around his fingers, a locket dangling from it in the glow of the candlelight. Handing it across the table, he placed it in her hand.

"Go ahead, open it," he said softly, waiting while she nervously worked the clasp. It took several attempts, but finally the locket fell open, causing Paige to gasp. On the left side, skillfully set inside the locket's cover, was a sparkling gold nugget. On the right was a simple inscription that said, "To Paige, for taking me above the bridge, Jake"

"Jake..." Paige whispered, her voice trailing off at a loss for words. "So does that mean..."

"No, I really did leave the gold there," Jake said slowly. "At least...I left...one rather tiny nugget, for sentimentality's sake. You know...the legend and all that."

"And the rest?" Paige asked, too surprised to even hide her curiosity.

"Oh, the rest?" Jake tapped his forehead, as if trying to remember what he did with it. Paige drummed her fingers on the table, barely able to handle the suspense. "Ah, the rest, now I remember." He leaned forward across the table and motioned with this finger for her to lean in, as well.

"Well, I'm not crazy, you know," he whispered. "Of course I kept the rest. Legends only carry so much weight." With that, Jake sat back, a grin on his face.

Paige laughed and shook her head in amazement as Jake waved for the bill. Paying it quickly, they stepped out onto the sidewalk. Soft lights glittered above shops and galleries. Small spotlights sent light filtering up into the trees. The neon sign of The Million Dollar Cowboy Bar cast a warm glow into the night air.

Jake slid his arm around Paige's shoulders as they walked across the street and into the town square. Stopping near the center, he reached for Paige's hand and lifted it, slowly uncurling her fingers, which still clutched the gold locket firmly inside. He took the locket and slid the delicate chain around her neck, fastening the clasp securely.

Together they breathed in the cool mountain air, crisp and clean as it filled their lungs. Muted conversation and laughter flowed across from the Million Dollar Cowboy Bar. A breeze rustled through the trees overhead, sending a few autumn leaves floating to the ground.

Paige turned briefly to glance around the square. For a split second she thought she saw a faint light coming from the antler arch, but when she blinked and looked again, it was dark. Just like the surrounding trees, the arch was simply a shadow in the night. Closing her eyes, she rested her head on Jake's shoulder, felt the warmth of his arms wrap around her and said a silent thank you for the magic of Jackson Hole.

ACKNOWLEDGEMENTS

I owe sincere thanks to so many people who helped bring this book into existence. I'm extremely grateful for the help of Carol Anderson, Jay Garner, Karen Putnam and Nancy Roessner, all gracious readers who provided insightful feedback on final drafts. Special appreciation is owed to Elizabeth Christy for her outstanding editorial assistance, as well as to Keri Knutson of Alchemy Book Covers and Tim Renfrow of Book Design and More. And big hugs go to my Wyoming "big sister," Mary Udy, who tolerated my never-ending obsession with getting this story written.

In addition, numerous research sources deserve thanks for the outstanding services they provide:

The Jackson Hole Historical Society and Museum is a gold mine of knowledge on area history. Shannon Sullivan, Curator of Collections, was especially helpful in providing valuable fact-checking expertise and access to photographic archives.

The Teton County Library's research section on local history provides a wealth of information on the history of Jackson Hole. Of particular help was the book, "A Place Called Jackson Hole: A Historic Resource Study of Grand Teton National Park," by John Daugherty, with contributions by Stephanie Crockett, William H. Goetzmann, and Reynold G. Jackson.

The National Museum of Wildlife Art offers top-notch educational resources about wildlife, ecology, art and western heritage, as well as an outstanding view of the National Elk Refuge.

The Craig Thomas Discovery and Visitor Center boasts a magnificent relief map of Jackson Hole, detailing near infinite possibilities for hiding - or discovering - hidden treasure.

Additional thanks go to many other family members and friends - you know who you are. Above all, I am grateful to Paul Sterrett and to my father, Bruce Garner, for believing in me. Without their patience, support and encouragement, this book would never have been written.

CPSIA information can be obtained at www.ICGtesting.com
Printed in the USA
LVOW13s1611040614

388614LV00006B/789/P